THE REMAINDER

Alia Trabucco Zerán

Translated by Sophie Hughes

SHEFFIELD – LONDON – NEW YORK

This edition first published in 2018 in the UK by And Other Stories
Sheffield – London – New York
www.andotherstories.org

First published as *La Resta* by Editorial Demipage in 2014
Copyright © Alia Trabucco Zerán, 2014
English-language translation © Sophie Hughes, 2018

9 8 7 6 5 4 3 2

ISBN: 978-1-911508-32-8
eBook ISBN: 978-1-911508-35-9

Editor: Anna Glendenning; Copy-editor: Saba Ahmed; Proofreader: Sarah Terry; Typesetter: Tetragon, London; Typefaces: Linotype Neue Swift and Verlag; Cover Design: Tree Abraham. Printed and bound by CPI Group (UK) Ltd, Croydon, CRO 4YY.

A catalogue record for this book is available from the British Library.

This book was supported using public funding by Arts Council England.

To my mother and father

Off and on: one week there, the next nowhere to be seen, that's how my dead began, out of control, every other Sunday then two in a row, catching me unawares in the strangest of places: lying at bus stops, on curbs, in parks, hanging from bridges and traffic lights, floating down the Mapocho, they were scattered all over Santiago those Sunday stiffs, weekly or bimonthly corpses which I totted up methodically, and the tally rose like foamy scum, like rage and lava it rose, till I twigged that adding them up was really the problem, because it makes no sense for the number to rise when we all know that the dead fall, they blame us, they drag us down, like this stiff I found slung out on the pavement just today, a solitary corpse waiting patiently for me to come by, and it just so happened that I was strolling down Bustamante, looking for a dive to have a beer and ride out the heat, this sticky heat that melts even the coldest calculations, so that's what I'm doing, gasping for a watering hole to cool off at, when on the corner of Rancagua I spot one of my pesky dead, all alone and still warm, still deciding whether to stay in this life or head into the next one, there he is, waiting for me in a hat and woollen coat, as if death lived in perpetual winter and he'd dressed for the occasion, right there with his head lolling, so I rush over to get a proper look at his eyes, bend down and lift his chin to catch him, to inspect him, to own him, and that's when I realise he has no eyes, no, just a pair of thick eyelids hiding him, eyelids like walls, like hoods, like wire fences, and I'm shaken up but I take a deep breath and I pull myself together, breathe out, crouch down and lick my thumb, wet it from top to bottom and hold it up to his face, and I gently raise his stiff eyelid, slowly draw back the curtain to spy on him, surround him, to subtract him, yeah, but a horrible fear pecks at my chest, a paralysing dread, cos his eye's swamped with a liquid that's not blue, or green, or brown, the eye peering back at me is black, a stagnant pool, a pupil that the night has clouded over, and I plunge to the depths of that socket and see myself, crystal clear, in the man's dark iris: drowned, defeated, broken in that watery tomb, but at least then I grasp the urgency, cos this corpse is a warning sign, a hint, a get-a-move-on, I see my face buried in his, my own eyes staring back at me from his sockets, and finally it clicks that I have to knuckle down, shake a leg if I'm going to get to zero, yeah, and just as I'm calming down and getting ready, just as I take out my pad to make a note of him, there, in the distance, is that unbearable wailing, the ambulance accelerating furiously, hurrying me as I subtract him, because adding them up is a big mistake, yeah, counting *up* is not the answer: how can I square the number of dead and the number of graves? how will I work out how many are born and how many remain? how can I reconcile the death toll with the actual sum of the dead? by deducting, tearing apart, rending bodies, that's it, by using this apocalyptic maths to finally, once and for all, wake up on that last day, grit my teeth and subtract them: sixteen million three hundred and forty-one thousand nine hundred and twenty-eight, minus three thousand and something, minus the one hundred and nineteen, minus one.

( )

That night it rained ash. Or perhaps it didn't. Perhaps the grey is just the backdrop of my memory and the rain I recall was, quite simply, rain.

The sun had already set and the whirlwind of hugs and kisses, of haven't-you-grown and how-time-flies had settled as evening fell. I had one very clear mission: to listen out for the doorbell, check thumbs for ink stains and, if all was in order, open the door. So seriously had I taken my mother's instructions ('that *key* role,' as she kept saying), that I'd felt compelled to give up my barbies, bury them in the back garden and at last assume my role as doorkeeper. I was all grown-up. I was going to be the one to guard the house, I thought, as I plunged the dolls into the soil, unaware that soon after I'd hand them down, black with dirt, to Felipe.

I dutifully carried out my job, greeting the stream of guests as euphoric as they were nervous, and who, having hesitated at the gate (the mud, the wild shrubs, the weeds invading the soil), let themselves be swept up in the revelries once inside. I remember all of this well but without a hint of nostalgia. I remember the damp smell of the earth, the tart berries on my tongue, the mud encrusting itself on my knees (turning me stiff, turning me to stone). Dusty memories shaken out, stripped of any yearning. I've learnt

9

to tame my nostalgia (I keep it tied to a post far away), and besides, I didn't choose to hold on to this memory. It was the fifth of October 1988, but it was my mother, not I, who decided that date would never be forgotten.

It was already late when I spotted three strangers walking up to the gate. Two giants and a regular-sized girl who took an unusually long time to find the bell. Eventually they called out a name, the wrong name, 'Claudia, Claudia,' they shouted hesitantly, watching their backs for any shadows that might be lurking. The girl was the only one who stayed silent and didn't move. Her blonde hair, her bored expression and the piece of gum hopping from one side of her mouth to the other gave her away as the guest my mother had told me about that morning ('get ready', 'say hello', 'make her welcome', 'smile nicely'). She didn't even look up when I opened the door. Standing stock-still, her eyes boring into her white espadrilles, hands buried inside her faded-jean pockets and a pair of headphones covering her ears – that's all it took, she had me. To her right a tall, blonde, bearded man ushered her in, his hand resting on her head (submerging her, burying her). And to her left, straight as an arrow, a stern-looking woman surveyed me, her face vaguely familiar, I thought, as if from an old photo, or a movie, but she interrupted me before I could put my finger on it.

'This is Paloma,' she said gesturing to the girl, shepherding her impatiently through the gate. 'And you must be Iquela? Give her a hug,' the woman ordered. Paloma and I did as we were told, feigning we knew each other, feigning a long-awaited reunion, feigning our parents' nostalgia.

Paloma seemed like a rock star to me. She refused to move from the hallway when we went inside the house and her parents didn't try to persuade her. They disappeared in a

merry-go-round of hugs, it's-been-so-long, I-don't-believe-it,
Ingrid's-here, and almost without my noticing it, Paloma and
I had been left on our own: two unflinching statues before
the parade of guests who flitted indecisively from the living
room to the kitchen, from the kitchen to the dining room,
from excitement to fear. Paloma was listening to music and
didn't seem to care about anything beyond her feet, which
were tapping along to a tune, jigging up and down furiously.
One, two, silence. One, two. I didn't know what to say to
her, how to interrupt her or overcome the shyness that had
left me with next to no fingernails. I'd got used to spending
my time with the grown-ups, and her mysterious presence,
announced by my mother as if she were heralding the arrival
of an angel or a Martian, had kept me on tenterhooks all day.
Completely mute, no doubt having been dragged against her
will to this lame party, the only bone Paloma threw me was
the beat of her heel against the floor. It was the only clue as
to what she was listening to, I thought, creeping one of my
feet towards hers and tapping along until I'd become part of
that inaudible chorus. She tapped two beats and I another
two. But soon after, with the pair of us almost dancing on the
spot, she froze; we both froze. Paloma turned and stood in
front of me, looming ten, maybe fifteen centimetres taller,
before taking my hand, turning my palm upwards and passing me her headphones.

'Place them on,' she said, with that clumsy turn of phrase
and strange accent. 'Place them on and put play,' she insisted,
still chewing on that squashed white worm. In the end
she wrapped the small black pillows around my ears herself, indicating with a finger against her lips that I should
follow her in silence. I walked alongside her, as close as I
could, hypnotised by the silky bra strap peeping out at her

11

shoulder, the tip of her plait like a fish hook hanging down at her waist, and that music coming from some corner of my mind: a guitar, a voice, the saddest lament in the world.

Trying at all costs to slip by unnoticed, Paloma and I tiptoed into the dining room. Wine glasses, tumblers, a mountain of newspapers, pamphlets and a battery-operated radio were spread the length and breadth of the table where my father and hers were patting each other on the back, touching one another's faces as if needing to confirm that their names really coincided with their bodies. On the radio, the programme my parents listened to every night was just about to start, the maniacal drum roll and familiar refrain announcing the beginning of an endless stream of bad news. It was the soundtrack to those years: the interminable era of the drums. I explained to Paloma that the radio wasn't old. It ran on batteries so that we were prepared, so that we wouldn't be caught short in the event of a power cut.

'During the blackouts, Felipe and I play Night-time,' I whispered, moving in closer towards her ear. 'We play at disappearing.'

I don't know whether Paloma didn't hear me or just pretended not to. She walked off and began to compare tumblers and wine glasses, picking them up and holding them to her nose before rejecting them with a look of disgust. Only two passed her ruthless selection process and ended up in front of me.

'White or pink?' she asked in her guttural voice.

'Pink,' I said. (Did she really say *pink*? Does the memory still count if I've forgotten my reply?)

Paloma handed me the glass of wine and took a tumbler of whisky for herself. 'Delicious,' she whispered, stirring the ice with her forefinger. 'Have it. Have the wine. Or don't you

like it, Iquela? How old are you?' she asked without blinking,
and I noticed hundreds of freckles dotted all over her face,
and under her eyebrows a pair of eyes so blue they looked
fake. Plastic eyes. False eyes that were judging me, exposing
me. She gave a well-rehearsed grin, a mechanical flash of
teeth, not even close to a real smile, and then she spat the
little worm into the palm of her hand and moulded it into
a ball between her forefinger and thumb.

'You first,' she said pointing at my glass. 'You drink,' she
insisted, still refusing to leave that slowly hardening round
mass in peace.

I took a deep breath, closed my eyes and, tilting my head
back, downed the wine in one, two, three torturous swigs.
I couldn't contain a shudder as I opened my eyes. Paloma
was polishing off her whisky, not a single hair raised. An
ice cube crunched between her teeth and she placed the
tumbler on the table, satisfied, cool as anything. Now she
really was smiling.

The guests were getting louder now, interrupting one
another, pacing frantically around the room, talking faster
and faster, producing more and more noise and fewer words.
The radio made itself heard among their voices: second
count of votes in. My mother was shuffling back and forth
nervously.

'What do you think?' she said into thin air, or to anyone
who felt inclined to answer. 'Will the military even respect
the outcome? Another drink anyone? More ice? Shall we
turn up the radio?' and then she let out a few tinny bursts
of laughter, a laugh I remember so well. I couldn't believe
those ear-piercing hoots were coming from my mother,
the slot of her open mouth (her bright white teeth a
cliff edge).

I didn't want Paloma to see her like that. I wanted to go up to her and say, 'Mum, I love you lots, lots and lots, be quiet. I'm begging you, shush, Mum, please.' But the drums on the radio drowned out her laughing, or her shrieks fell into rhythm with that drumming, which told us it was time to be quiet, to settle down and listen to the results, 72 per cent of the votes counted.

With the news bulletin now over and no more alcohol left on the table, Paloma announced to me that she wanted to smoke. She took my hand and led me along the hallway. I remember we were swaying. A new kind of excitement was rushing through me, a giddy sensation that Paloma interrupted just a few steps later.

'And your cigarettes?' she asked with one of her floppy 'R's, gripping my hand and looking at me with those eyes that left me no choice but to shut up and do as she told me.

I led her to my parents' room at the back of the house, where the din of the party barely reached us. Paloma went in and began to comb every inch of the bedroom, without even looking behind her first. I, on the other hand, clamped my eyes shut and closed the door (shut your eyes to shut out the world, so that no one can see you). When I opened them again, Paloma was waiting impatiently for me.

'So?'

I pointed to the nightstand. That's where my mother kept her cigarettes, matches and the pills she took sometimes, on the occasional grey day and without fail on blackout nights. There was only one cigarette left in her packet of Barclays, but Paloma opened the drawer, rummaged through it and removed a fresh one. She also took a pack of pills, and all these things vanished inside a red purse which had appeared as if by magic, hanging from her shoulder (because this is the kind of detail you do remember: the glare of a red purse).

The floor began to shift beneath my feet, a lazy rolling motion like the sea, which I navigated uneasily, happy yet fretful, as Paloma and I zigzagged our way through the house. Together we passed the hallway and the living room, and together we left behind the murmur of voices and the latest count, 83 per cent of the votes now in. I gripped her hand as tightly as I could and led her outside, away from where our fathers were shouting at one another. Her father had stood up from his chair and mine was hiding behind his reading glasses, the ones that split his face in two.

Leaning against the wall, my father used a knife to clink his glass. Ding, ding, ding. Silence. Ding, ding. It was as if that sound might protect him from the German's wrath, which seemed to have been brewing for years, ready to be released in that very moment. 'A minute's silence,' my father called out, achieving the desired hush, a pause he used to raise a toast to a whole catalogue of strangers, a list of people with two names and two surnames, as tradition dictated we refer to the dead.

I closed the sliding door to the front garden behind me and Paloma and I stood there in the darkness and silence (was it ash coming down, or was it raining?). The lights had gone out, and the grown-ups had only just noticed everything had turned black: 'power cut', 'someone's brought the line down', 'turn up the radio' (and I thought about my mother and her pills, her pills). Paloma lit a candle and removed the packet of Barclays from her purse.

'We'll have a cigarette?' she asked, her R falling flat, before she carefully removed the wrapper from the box. She pulled out the golden paper inside, threw it on the ground and tapped the packet twice with the palm of her hand. Two cigarettes popped out. I took mine between my forefinger and middle finger, imitating my mother when she smoked. Paloma, on the other hand, raised the packet to her mouth, took the filter in her lips and drew the cigarette towards her as if it were incredibly fragile. Then, dipping her head, she brushed the tip of the cigarette against the candle's flame. A professional. The flame lit up her eyes and she inhaled, squinting (red eyes, I thought, pink eyes). The tobacco glowed and a white, dense smoke hung in the air, millimetres from her lips. I watched her, fascinated and jealous, 88 per cent of the votes counted, as that haze emerged from her mouth and immediately dissolved around her.

I was in awe and asked her to teach me. How did she know all those moves? How long had she smoked for? How did she do it without coughing? 'You have never smoked?' she asked, taking another drag. 'But you have tried these pills before, no?' she said, popping one of the capsules out of its pack and placing it on her tongue, still shrouded in billows of smoke.

I felt a nervous flutter in my stomach and a burning in my chest and face. I replied that I hadn't, no, of course I'd never smoked.

'It's gross,' I said, concentrating on a fixed spot on the floor, a different spot to the one she'd stared at when she first turned up at our house. I studied the ground looking for something beyond her espadrilles, beyond my feet and the soil, beyond myself, a secret I couldn't unearth. I told her she would end up with black nails, dull skin and yellow teeth. And those pills were for my mum, for the grey days, for blackout nights. She ignored me and carried on talking, telling me how she smoked every morning before school in

16

Berlin with her friends. I didn't know where Berlin was, but I imagined her blowing those clouds of smoke through an enormous pale-green forest, and I hated her.

Inside the house the lights had come back on and the radio was on full blast, drowning out our conversation. Paloma's dad was going ballistic, yelling and wagging his finger at my father.

'Fucking grass. Squealer. Don't you dare raise your glass to them, you son of a bitch.'

My mother walked into the living room just then, and on finding Hans ranting at my father she picked up the first glass she saw, refilled it, and went over to him, holding it in front of herself as if it were a shield, putting a translucent distance between them, begging him with that pink wine to calm down.

'Please, it's not worth it, Hans. Let's have a drink, eh? Let's celebrate the good news. What good will it do now, after everything? Today's a special day, Hans,' she said, forcing the wine on him and managing to tame his irate finger. 'Some things are better left unsaid.'

Paloma's mother was watching the scene unfold from an armchair, nodding her head and wearing what seemed to me a strange expression, as if only now, amid all the shouting and votes, from inside the eye of all that rage, did she truly recognise my mother (Claudia? Consuelo? not even she knew). My father, on the other hand, was crestfallen and mute. He looked as if he wanted to say something, smoke a cigarette, listen to music till he fell asleep (the ends of his feet poking out of a blanket, the gentle whirr of the TV), but the German was on the attack again – 'Fucking snitch!' – and my father's voice seemed to be trapped. I wanted to hug him, to protect him from it all. A new kind of silence had grown between Paloma and me, which I broke when I couldn't stand the shouting any more.

'I want to smoke, too,' I said, 93 per cent of the votes counted. 'I'm going to get out of here with you,' I added, unaware that this promise would go unfulfilled for so many years.

Paloma turned her back to the sliding door, took out the little box of matches, lit one and held it up to my mouth.

'We will just smoke,' she said ('Cigarette?' she would learn to say in time). 'It's important,' she added, jiggling the cigarette between her lips.

I nodded, wanting to ask her how to do it, if my chest would hurt, if the smoke would burn, if I would suffocate on the inside. But the flame was going out before my eyes and there was no time for questions.

I inhaled deeply and without another thought.

I inhaled and my throat clamped shut like a fist.

I inhaled just as my mother came out of the sliding door, looking for me.

Paloma jumped and drew away.

I hid the cigarette behind my back and for a second, as my mother approached, I managed to hold in both the smoke and my coughing fit. My mother crouched down and looked me in the eyes. The smoke in my chest was desperately looking for an exit. She hugged me and held on tight, and I heard thousands of votes being counted, I felt the cigarette burning between my fingers, I saw Paloma's giant of a father striding towards mine, and felt the smoke pushing and pushing. My mother held me by the shoulders, dug her nails into my skin and spoke to me between sniffles, her voice cracking like the branches of a dead tree.

'Iquela, my girl, don't ever forget this day.' (Because I mustn't forget anything, ever.) 'Don't ever forget,' she repeated, and the dry cough finally burst out of me. It rose up and shook me till I was completely hollowed out.

The air had cooled and it felt like the taste of wine, like berries, like Paloma's Rs. A thick, harsh air, a closed sky. As soon as my mother left, Paloma came back over to me. She rubbed my back, patted it a few times and then placed three pills in the palm of my hand (a bright white ellipsis). Then she took out another three, which immediately disappeared into her mouth.

'Take them,' she said, as if inviting me to be part of a secret ritual. 'Take them, quick,' she insisted, and I took them without thinking while Paloma held my face in her hands.

I swallowed the pills, despite how bitter they were, despite how afraid I was, as she leant in towards me and closed her eyes (hundreds of eyes that couldn't see me). I closed mine, wanting to play Night-time, Blackout, to play at disappearing. I closed my eyes and tried to picture those endless pale-green forests shrouded in the haze flowing from her mouth. I wasn't expecting the kiss. It lasted barely a few seconds, neither rushed nor lingering, just long enough for Paloma and I to catch the exact moment her father punched mine, for my coughing fit to return and drown out the final count of votes, and for me to watch as my mother hugged someone else, so that they, too, would never forget that day.

It's someone's turn to croak and it's my job to find them, body after body, ever since that first, unforgettable Sunday cadaver, that trailblazing corpse who changed everything, yeah, cos he was waiting for me to subtract him, staring up from the ground with his big brown eyes, and I stared right back and it was love at first sight: I knew that corpse in the Plaza de Armas belonged to me, of course, but that's not to say I go around looking for bodies, hell no, they find me, no matter what others might think, my Gran Elsa, for example, who would always say people see what they want to see, Felipito, and by the looks of things I want to see corpses, because from that day on they've kept cropping up, always uninvited, be it a weekday, holiday or even New Year's, because at first it was Sundays, that's true, but now they crop up whenever they like, one after the other, so I'm strolling through Yungay minding my own business, stumbling along in the heat, when I spot a guy doubled up like a contortionist on the curb, head slumped between his knees, neck twisted, and looking like that anyone would assume he's a drunk, the dregs of that weekend's party, or just one more soul who's had enough of this godawful heat, but no, it's a corpse, and then I only have to get on the bus to spot that the man sitting at the back, the one with his cheek pressed against the window, isn't leaving any breath on the glass, no, he's dead too; I only have to focus my gaze a little, be hawk-eyed, cow-eyed, owl-eyed, to see them everywhere, it's just a matter of dilating the pupils I have all over my body, to see that the man waiting at the bus stop sure is going to be late, yeah, he's kicked the bucket too, because that's how they make themselves known: no warning, no fuss, and I make a note in my pad, in fives I subtract them, and have been doing since day one, since that first one appeared as I was roaming around the Plaza de Armas watching the rats eat discarded peanuts as the sun went down, that's what I was doing, sniffing black flowers in the blackest of nights, trying to shake off the day's thoughts, when suddenly I spotted something strange in the middle of the square, there where the gallows used to be, where they used to hang the non-believers, the thieves, the traitors, I noticed something odd there and I moved in, yeah, and for a moment I thought it was a stray dog having a nap and I sidled up to say hello, but once I reached it I realised it was something else, a man or a woman, or maybe a man and a woman in one, that's what I thought, and I noticed that the poor soul was sprawled out on his back like only a dead soul would be, dislocated, stiff, silent as the grave that tall dead man in a thick chequered skirt, argyle socks, a pair of blue rubber flip-flops and with a red handkerchief tied around his head, there he was with that wide face of his, and yet he had no face, his eyes had shrunk back under his skin, had gone into hiding, yeah, and I stood staring at him and at those pigeons, because there were twelve pigeons holding a vigil for him, cooing dirges in unison, and there were also fleas all over his socks, and rats and stray dogs sniffing around him and whimpering, and I was scared but not too scared because at least it was night-time and not the middle of the day: everyone knows we think differently at night, and I was thinking about how that square wasn't a bad place to die, the place where it all begins and ends, that's what I was thinking, but then I got distracted remembering how, when I was a kid, at least they warned you on TV if a dead body was coming on the screen, when the blonde on Channel 7 would say 'the following images are not suitable for sensitive people or minors', that's what the skinny blonde would say, and my Gran Elsa must have been pretty sensitive because she would cover her eyes with her wrinkly hands, cover her entire face with those tree trunk hands and rock herself back and forth until the horridness had gone away, but she didn't say a word to me, no, and I would sit there crouched in front of the TV staring at dead people in the ground, or rather at their bones, a layer cake of bones at the bottom of a hole, hundreds of skeletons keeping each other company, keeping each other warm, rubbing up against each other, and me with my big eyes, I thought they were lovely those beautiful white bones, because I loved the colour white, osso buco-white, of course, because I loved osso buco, with its greyish-white gelatinous marrow, exactly the white of our bath in Chinquihue, the filthy tub I would climb into after the news to turn myself white and disappear, opening the cold water full blast, stripping and slipping in butt naked to study my feet as I waited for my toenails to go white, but they never went white, no, they went blue: my toes blue under the icy water, my skin goose pimply and, after a while, wrinkly like dates, like elephants, like old tomatoes, my own shell about to shed itself, my skin trying to peel away, and that's exactly what I wanted under that cold water there in Chinquihue, I wanted to peel away from myself, but I couldn't, because my Gran Elsa would turn up just in time to say, what in God's name are you doing in there, give me strength, you're growing more feral by the day, and then she'd pull me, trembling and numb from the water and with cold needles stabbing me all over, and my gran would squeeze me and rub me down with a white towel, them bones, them bones, them dancing bones, all the while warning me that if I didn't stop misbehaving she'd take me to Iquela's in Santiago, and in Santiago the sticky heat and stench of sadness were waiting for me, as were those sourpusses Consuelo and Rodolfo, Rodolfo with that scar across his middle, and then, despite the whiteness of the towel, those night-time thoughts would come flooding back, mad ants all over my scalp, yeah, and my gran would thrash the black thoughts with the towel, shoo them away saying, you feral child, that's what my Gran Elsa would say as she rubbed me down, smoothing out my skin, ironing out the skin rolled up over my bones, my skinny bones, which were obvious even from beneath my clothes, just like the bones jutting out of those graves in the ground, the bones that were always on TV, yeah, but with prior warning at least, not like now when they pop out of nowhere, one after the other they appear, the dead of Santiago, this mortuary city which I'm sure as hell is neither sensitive nor a minor.

( )

The phone caught me off guard. I was in the middle of translating an untranslatable sentence into Spanish, stiff from several hours spent sitting in the same armchair, when that dreadful ringing began. If it had been nine fifteen in the morning I would have known who it was. She had an unwavering timetable: the stroke of nine fifteen, every day. But at three in the afternoon, it simply couldn't be my mother. I stopped what I was doing but went on thinking about how the translation had me cornered. There was a mistake in the original English and I was debating whether to translate the sentence as it stood or correct it: to translate the error faithfully, reproducing it in the Spanish, or inaccurately, adapting the original. So, still struggling with this dilemma, and with pins and needles beginning to creep up my leg, I picked up the phone.

She spoke very slowly, calculating precise pauses between each breath and her words. No niceties or remarks on the weather, the godawful heat: nothing to cushion the bad news. She used that urgent voice which came so naturally to her, hammering home each syllable, driving the message right into the back of my head.

'She's-dead,' (and a sinking sensation: a stream of pets, friends, family, all dead). 'In-grid-is-dead.'

I said nothing while I tried to put a face to that name, to put a face to the profile: Ingrid, Ingrid. Of course I remembered her: one of the tall, slim giants ringing our doorbell all those years ago. Breaking the long, tense silence, I finally told my mother that I didn't have the first idea who Ingrid was. I'd managed to wind her up in record time and she snapped that the daughter was landing in Santiago the following day, and I was to use her car to go and collect her from the airport. My mother couldn't be expected to leave the house in this heat.

'Her name's Paloma,' she said to herself. 'You and your memory. Like a sieve.'

I sweated all the way to the airport. Really, I hadn't stopped sweating for the last few weeks, but now cooped up in my mother's car, the heat was unbearable. And it wasn't just the air inside the car. Through the windows a dense, warm breeze slipped in: breath from the mouths of strangers swimming towards mine. I closed the windows and dabbed the beads gathering on my forehead and neck. It was hellish. There hadn't been a drop of rain in months and the heat had dug its claws into Santiago with no apparent intention of yielding. At least, when it had begun, the papers had honoured it with headlines. 'HEATWAVE DEVASTATES CROPS', 'AGRICULTURAL CATASTROPHE IN CENTRAL CHILE'. But, by mid-autumn, the thirty-six point six, point seven, point eight degrees creeping up the thermometers was no longer news. Everyone seemed to have grown used to the eternal summer. Everyone except me. I still made a point of chasing the shade if I had to go out, snaking my way along pavements, dashing from trees to awnings despite knowing full well that the problem wasn't the sun. The source of the heat, that malign heat, came from somewhere else. It was subterranean. It pushed and peeled the crust off pavements. It smothered you from your feet upwards. That heat was a warning that the ash was on its way. But I couldn't have cared less about the ash. In fact, I quite liked the grey rinse over the parks and gardens, the grey settling on the roofs and houses. I found it soothing, even. The tough part was the build-up, the wait. The heat was my real nightmare. Or worse: it was a sign of the nightmare to come.

The airport arrivals hall filled and emptied several times as I waited, listening to music, reliving my first encounter with Paloma and idly watching what was going on around me: the looks of anticipation whenever the doors slid open, the bureaucratic smiles of the hostesses, the mechanical, penguin-like shuffle people made as they leant on one leg and then the other. All those friends-and-relatives stuck in that hall, tired from standing and from all that nervous anticipation, but also, somehow, savouring the sweet wait. They were men and women used to waiting (in airports, hospitals, courtrooms, at bus stops).

It really made no sense for me to stand there going over that old promise, the promise of getting out, of myself leaving some day, which hadn't waned since Paloma's first visit. The illusions I'd entertained over the subsequent years were no more than hazy fantasies involving some mode of transport or another: the last seat in a train carriage; my outstretched thumb on a long empty highway. I'd planned that journey like you'd plan an escape: the destination had never mattered. The bottom line was to get out. To get out of Santiago at all costs. I had enough savings to travel a thousand or so kilometres in any direction, but still the only road I'd ever taken in my life was the eight and a half blocks to my mother's house.

I peered through the sliding doors one last time to try to see beyond them, already anticipating the earful I'd get from my mother – my indolence, my impatience – when I dropped her car back without Paloma. I didn't expect to see anything through those doors. I told myself that, having failed to recognise me among the crowd, she must have decided to make her own way to the house. And then, there she was.

A group of taxi drivers pounced on her with boards and questions she seemed not to hear. There was Paloma, a small suitcase in one hand and a lit cigarette in the other. Her blonde hair was scraped up in a messy bun and she was in shorts and a white T-shirt, which she fanned up and down in an effort to cool down. She was smoking right in front of a policeman, who seemed not to believe his eyes and to be debating whether to fine her or let her do as she pleased. And she just puffed away, as though it were nothing. Her features had lost the roundness of youth, but her forehead was still covered in tiny freckles (several faces faded in and out on the same skin: Paloma as a little girl, Paloma the adult, the little girl again, and now her dead mother). Her eyebrows were darker than her hair, and a lick of mascara accentuated the contours of those eyes, which I'd imagined would be tired and bloodshot. Instead, she seemed calm. Too calm. As if nobody had died, or as if she were still on the plane looking out over the city nestled between the mountains, Paloma took hold of her camera, an old device suspended from her neck, and photographed an advert on the wall. She seemed rested, relaxed even, as she stared at that bottle of pisco – red, orange, green, purple: it changed colour depending on where you stood. Paloma raised herself on tiptoes, crouched down and then stood up straight again, and she repeated this several times trying to find the best possible angle. One of the taxi drivers, a fat, sweaty fellow, couldn't take his eyes off her strange little ritual. I made my way over to intervene, and as I approached – walking gradually faster and with more resolve – I was surprised by how clearly I remembered that furrowed brow, the dimples at the edge of her mouth, the grace with which she moved from one action to the next: fanning herself, taking a photo, smoking a cigarette.

The taxi driver pretended to receive an incoming call and disappeared among all the other people waiting in the arrivals hall. Paloma finally peeled her eyes from the bottle of pisco. She was sweating. A loose blonde lock had swept across her forehead and lent her a scruffy, unsettled sort of air, which she wouldn't lose over the days to come. She took a drag on her cigarette and shot me a vacant look: total indifference. And it was that gesture, that look, that pushed me to take the last few steps and throw myself at her. Paloma put out an arm just in time. Leaning back in a subtle but unmistakable recoil, she patted me on the shoulder, gracefully dodging my overenthusiastic hug.

'Iquela,' she said, as if speaking my name were part of a ritual, or as if the very word evoked another kind of ghost-like presence. I felt as if I'd taken a non-existent step on the stairs. Paloma, on the other hand, didn't bat an eyelid. She stubbed out her cigarette and thanked me for picking her up.

'I thought Consuelo was coming,' she said with a cordial smile, her eyes (those false eyes, lying eyes) resting on a fixed spot beyond my face, beyond the airport, beyond the city where she still hadn't quite touched down.

Paloma sounded strange to me when she spoke. Perhaps I was waiting for the voice she'd had as a little girl, that grating tone that still lurked in my memory but was nothing like the accent she now answered my questions with. I thought she would still speak her clumsy Spanish from '88. But she had learnt to swallow whole consonants and syllables, to inhale her 'S's as if it hurt to say them, to fill gaps in the conversation with remarks on the heat or smog, to try to avoid silences just as I did: unsuccessfully. Because as soon as the obligatory hellos and questions were over with, a great long pause opened up between us, the ideal opportunity for me to bring up her mother and return her cold pat on the shoulder. *I can't imagine what you must be going through. My condolences. I'm so sorry for your loss.* Each commiseration I thought of sounded worse than the one before – cold and way too formal, like a poor translation.

I got through the silence by compiling a mental list of all the objects around us. This way, my eyes wouldn't give away how uncomfortable I felt (and I counted twelve suitcases being pulled along by exhausted figures, one pearl necklace holding up a double chin, two cardboard signs announcing foreign-sounding surnames, and three flights: one delayed, one diverted, one cancelled).

My list was left half-finished. Paloma tapped my shoulder and asked what I was thinking about. It was the kind of question my mother would have asked; the kind of question people might have asked Paloma when she zoned out or fell silent. You couldn't just land, say hello and expect to know what somebody was thinking. I didn't answer. Answering her wasn't on my mental list, which was already collapsing inside my head. But then again, my question about where they kept the coffin on the plane, which was the only thing I wanted to know, the only thing I could think of saying upon seeing that small suitcase at her feet, didn't feel like the most appropriate conversation starter.

Instead, I told her we'd have dinner at my mother's house at eight. If she preferred, we could go and drop her things off first so she didn't have to lug them around for the rest of the day. Paloma just pointed at her neat little trolley and told me not to go to any trouble, but she repeated that she thought it strange that Consuelo hadn't come to the airport.

'On the phone she told me she would come personally to pick me up,' she said, lisping a little, as if her 'S's were obstructed by something in her tongue (a screw, an arrow, a rusty nail). 'She promised me,' she went on, and now I couldn't stop staring at that shiny barbell and how it plunged right into her tongue. 'Has something happened to Consuelo? Is she OK?'

I finally managed to peel my eyes from her tongue (and I counted three cigarette butts on the floor). I nodded without looking up. Of course my mother was OK. That wasn't the issue. The reason she hadn't come herself had more to do with who exactly was included in her version of 'personally', in the 'I' of her 'I'll pick you up'. But I didn't say any of this to Paloma. Instead, I suggested we take a drive around Santiago before eating. We had bags of time before dinner, which was sure to be excruciating.

My routine visits to my mother's house were always brief, as if we'd just bumped into each other on the corner and I had something terribly important to do a few blocks away. Nine fifteen a.m.: the telephone rings. Nine twenty: buy the paper, buy some fresh bread, buy a little more time. Nine forty: walk the eight and a half blocks to find her, without fail, drenching the lawn, the flagstones, the chipped wicker furniture in the front garden. And then our series of false starts would begin: we would be talking and my mother would start cooking or doing her make-up; we would be talking and my mother would water the plants or put away the shopping; we would be talking and my mother would start reminiscing, forcing me to stay another twenty minutes, half an hour, forty minutes, which would drag painfully slowly as she repeated the same old stories, her emphases and regrets always unchanged. We rarely spoke facing each other, and even more rarely over dinner. My eyes were the problem; I didn't know how to hold that gaze, how to bear the weight of all those things she'd seen. Instead, I focused on her thin lips and the picture-hook scars on the wall. And if I made myself look her in the eye, if I took a deep breath and managed to hold that gaze for even a second, my mother never missed her chance: 'You have my eyes, Iquela. Every day you look more and more like me.' (And my eyes would plummet back down to the floor from the sheer weight of it all.)

As if she could already sense the tension of our approaching dinner, or her body were steeling itself for it, the moment we got into the car Paloma began to jiggle one of her legs madly. I made no attempt to placate her. Next, she set about tuning the radio, flicking from station to station, and finally she wound the window up and down, all the while chain-smoking: cigarette after cigarette, the next one lit with the glowing tip of the last. She only loosened up when she remembered her phone and managed to hook it up to the radio. A slow, sad song seemed to soothe her (a woman, a guitar, a wordless melody). I drove, paying more attention to what she was up to than taking the best route, the least congested one. Then, perhaps hoping to delay that impending meal, to get lost and turn up late maybe, or to boycott it altogether, I changed

31

direction suddenly and suggested that we drive to see the city from above.

'You get the best of Santiago from outside Santiago,' I said, putting my foot down and not waiting for a response.

No matter how many people are around, or who passes through the same place, it's always me who finds them, my hundreds of eyes opening wide to spot them, not like Iquela, who never catches a thing, who just drifts about commenting on the dappled sunlight through the plum trees or the way the shadows of the buildings stretch out across the ground, and I just nod, aha, I say, hmm, wow, would you look at that, Ique, but I never notice those things myself, I never see pretty or bright or ordinary things, just as she never sees anything ugly or rare or important; she doesn't see the dead, for instance, or that old fellow over there on Avenida 10 de Julio, the one pissing into a bottle of ginger ale and telling the world that his piss has come out all fizzy, no, Iquela just prattles on about the golden earth at dusk, and I mean, give me a break! but I don't say that to her, no, cos if we fall out, who's going to lend me their sofa when I'm broke in Santiago? and so I go along with it and I say, hmm, yeah, beautiful Ique, and we take our strolls through the city, me stomping on the crispest, brownest leaves, and Iquela telling me shush, stop that Felipe! because the little princess wants silence, shut up, she says, as if that precious golden floor can only be fully appreciated by our little Buddha, and the problem is Iquela always goes around like that, as serious as a heart attack, whereas I, I flit about, cos too much silence makes me jumpy, ever since I was a little boy I've always preferred noise, yeah, a real racket to muffle the chatter in my head, and that's why I listen to music, I just pop my headphones on and voila, a miracle cure, but after two or three hours the batteries die so then what I do is crunch brown crispy leaves, and as I crunch them I think of crisp, crunchy things to see if the sound of those thoughts drown out the ones already in my head, and this leads me straight back to my gran sitting in the kitchen in Chinquihue, Granny Elsa and the sound of eggshells being crushed between her fingers, because you had to mix the crushed shells with the milk, one dash of milk to one generous hand-ful of shells to feed the emaciated mutt, to keep up his calcium, she would say, and the shell would go crunch and she'd mix it with the milk and give it to the lonesome little pup, to the half-starved mongrel who had turned up at our door one morning, all floppy-eared and wet-nosed, trembling because the mummy-pup didn't want him any more, the mummy-pup had gone, and the daddy-pup, well, that was anyone's guess, my gran said, cradling him in her hands, and I knew right away that she was going to love him, because my Gran Elsa loved everyone like a son: the dog, the hens, Evaristo the parrot, and me, of course, she even told me to call her Mum, Mamushka, Mummakins, but I was too feral to call her anything, so all I did was silently watch my brother-pup as he lapped up his milk, how he dipped his spongy tongue into the curd, yeah, and I loved watching that wet tongue, I loved watching it lap up the milk as it poured with rain, and the rain sank down into the mud, into the tiles, into me, and the mongrel's nails sank into the rug, and my eyes sank into his furry coat, and the little pup spluttered as he lapped up his milk, yeah, and I spluttered too so that he and I were alike, we spluttered together in a chorus of animal splutters, and then my gran would try and convince me to eat, because I didn't like hard-boiled eggs, man, how I hated those eggs! and there it was, once again, the perennial egg on my plate, that's disgusting, Gran! especially the white, so smooth, so soft, and I don't like smooth things, but if my brother-pup could get even the shells down him, then I could eat my egg too, that's how Granny Elsa would persuade me and it's her I think about whenever I walk along crunching the dry leaves of Santiago; I think about noisy things like the rain in Chinquihue and the stems of *nalcas* being chomped between my teeth, the strings of dried *piure* banging against the wall and logs collapsing in firesides, and I think about Evaristo the parrot locked up in his cage in the kitchen, noisy on the outside and silent on the inside, Shut that parrot up! Granny Elsa would say, and in the end it was he who showed me the true key to maths, how it all has an order, cos the order changes the product, the parts and the whole are two different things, and Evaristo would watch me with his tiny dilated eye, and if I moved he'd follow me, if I hid he'd trap me, my reflection locked up in that eye, and to be perfectly honest I loved it, I enjoyed seeing myself uprooted in there, I liked it so much that I wanted to see from closer up, to see myself from his point of view, and that's why, one day, I put my hand in the cage, just a little at first, then a little bit more, and Evaristo retreated, just a little, then a little bit more, until he was backed right up against the cold bars, the rigid grey bars of his tiny cage, at which point I grabbed him and felt his warm little body, his soft feathers and his panic-stricken flapping, because the poor parrot didn't want to leave, no, but I had no choice, I

had to either prove or disprove my hypothesis, that's what
Iquela's teachers at school would tell us, hypotheses must
be proved or disproved, boys and girls, so I grabbed him
tight, and he clamped his wings to his body and began to
screech, naturally, which is why, when I think noisy thoughts,
Evaristo comes to mind, that rowdy little thing, screeching
and shrieking as I carried him to my room in Chinquihue,
far enough away from my gran so that she couldn't hear,
and there we were, Evaristo and I, and I spent a long time
staring at him, finally getting to know him, because it didn't
matter what people looked like on the outside, that's all
superficial stuff, my boy, Gran would say, it's what's on the
inside that counts, son, and so I began to pluck Evaristo;
slowly I plucked each one of his feathers, his soft and green
and superficial feathers, yeah, I stripped him little by little,
placing them one by one on the table, and he was warm and
silent as the grave, cos it turns out that Evaristo was quiet
on the inside, that's what I thought as I arranged the feathers in a fan that was big and green and mine, I thought about
how there was a lot more on the inside than I'd imagined,
things like his screeching voice, his thoughts, and each and
every one of his bones, yeah, that's what I wanted to see the
most, his bones, so I sank the tip of a sharp fork into the
nape of his neck and a stream of blood came gushing out,
blood that was red and bright and beautiful, and right at
the bottom I saw his tiny bones, and his bones were also
red, because it's not true that bones are white, no, they're
red, bright red, and that's why nobody ever finds what they're
looking for, because they don't even know what that is, and
nor do they know that it's futile trying to reveal the whole,
yeah, it's the parts that count, that's what I thought as I
stared at the feathers splayed out like a green, circular fan,

and at the reddish puddle and wrinkly skin on my table, I wondered what I might need to put the parts back together, to reassemble the whole and return Evaristo to his cage; what was missing? what was missing? . . . what was missing was his voice, that's it, Pretty Polly!, because he was so quiet there, and I'm not really one for silence, and only then did I realise that I didn't know where it was, I'd lost Evaristo's voice, and there's no such thing as a bird without a voice, no, I couldn't put him back together again, so I mopped up all the feathers and skin and that lovely, crystalline blood, I put it in a shoebox and left the house, I went outside and wandered aimlessly in the middle of nowhere, I carried him in his cardboard box to where the cows were grazing, that's what I did, with my brother-pup hot on my heels, almost clipping my heels, and together we chose a lovely spot, a perfect spot, and we collapsed to the ground, yeah, and the mutt and I dug a big hole, he with his paws and I with my hands, on our knees we dug a deep hole, as deep as the one I'd seen on TV, a huge grave among the wild basil and mint, and there, at the bottom, we lay Evaristo's parts before covering them with dirt and moss and leaves, a big mound of wet earth, and only then did I feel a pang of sadness, a black, sticky pain that forced me to shut my eyes and feel the whiteness in my head, the whiteness bursting behind my eyes, the white pain of the lines in my mind's eye, random horizontal lines, dashes that read minus, minus, minus, yeah, and my brother-pup started to get restless and to howl at my side, and that lingering howl, that piercing cry was his first word, a pretty, pained howl which I echoed as loudly as I could, cos I wanted to howl too, and the howling made my eyes well up with salty tears, tears at the sad fact that the whole wasn't the same as the parts, because it turned out you can be red and silent on the inside even if you're green and shrill on the outside, and because, if I really think about it, Evaristo was my first dead; it was Evaristo, not that stranger in the Plaza de Armas, because, man or beast, dead means dead, and when we come across the dead we have to howl, that's right, howl until we have no voice left, until there's nothing left.

( )

Stale, muggy air. That was the first thing I noticed on entering my mother's house. The windows were closed with the
curtains drawn, the hallway was plunged in darkness and
in the dining room a lone lamp shining on a wilted bunch
of flowers completed the grim effect of studied dilapidation.

Paloma followed me to the table, sat down at my usual
place and began to talk easily, as if the only thing that had
been making her feel uncomfortable was the warm hug my
mother had just given her. Paloma had gone in for a stony pat
on the back, a reserved and formal 'Hello, Consuelo', but my
mother had clutched her in a tight embrace the moment we'd
walked in the front garden (tensed shoulders, tart berries,
feet tapping against the floor). Only after a minute had my
mother pulled away from a half-irritated, half-dumbfounded
Paloma to peer at her with the same disappointed look she
had so often given me; as if I were a hopelessly broken thing.

'Identical,' she declared, releasing Paloma's chin from
her grip. 'Apart from the eyes, you're identical to Ingrid,'
(and by 'eyes' she meant 'hollow, vacant eyes').

Now having recovered from this greeting, with a glass
of wine on the table in front of her and my mother a few
blessed metres away, Paloma seemed cheerier, perhaps even
glad to be able to use her Spanish, which was becoming

less rusty by the minute. She reeled off a list of cities where she'd lived as a child: Munich, Frankfurt, Hamburg, Berlin (and I hated her for all those adventures, for having left so many times). She spoke about Ingrid, about their numerous relocations, about what life out there had been like (out where? I wasn't sure).

'Her dream was always to come back to Chile,' Paloma told my mother, who shuffled back and forth from the kitchen to the dining room with water and wine, feigning indifference. 'And I don't know why she didn't, because she never stopped going on about you all,' she went on, inspecting the palms of her hands as if a belated and heartfelt apology might be hiding there.

I sat down opposite her, in Felipe's place from back when we were kids, and it was from this new vantage point that I noticed a change in the room. The dozens of tiny nails in the wall were no longer there, nails that used to remind me of the pictures my mother had taken down because of the tremors, the earthquakes. 'Who knows when the next one's going to hit, Iquela. Take them all down, I'm begging you,' she'd said, and all the walls had been left riddled with scars, which to me had become a kind of blueprint for the house. Now, in their place, hung unfamiliar landscapes: a bird glowing against a grey sky, a forest in the foothills of a mountain range.

My mother left the house more often than she was prepared to admit, and she let me know by leaving little clues like these new paintings, or those drooping roses on the table: foreign flowers from out there, roses that my mother had got without my help. So much for her declaration that she would never leave the house again: 'I'm only safe indoors,' she'd said, gnawing the skin around her nails. She no longer went to parties or invited anyone over. Except me, and I visited her three or four times a week, like clockwork, to appease her, to tell her 'nothing's going to happen out there, Mother' (although accidents happened, mistakes happened, and time passed).

And so, with perfect composure, my mother set the table for our meal, her body immune, as ever, to the heat. She had done herself up and her grey bob hung neatly just above her collarbones. Clearly, she was relishing having us – a captive audience – at home. Her lips were almost trembling with the effort of containing her smile, a strange smirk which I tried and failed to read: it was neither happy nor serious, genuine nor fake. It was as if a face behind her real face were happy, or as if her younger face, Consuelo's face, had reappeared from nowhere to welcome her friend Ingrid, not Paloma.

Now seated at the table, draping a napkin across her knees, my mother lectured Paloma for having let too much time pass. Her voice was full of reproach, and she over-pronounced each syllable to make sure that Paloma had understood what she had said; as if she hadn't just heard Paloma's fluent tales of various relocations; as if Paloma hadn't learnt a word of Spanish since 1988. And it was this presumption that made her adjust her voice, eking out the words until they broke into meaningless syllables: to-oo-mu-cha-time-ma. Paloma seemed pleased with her Spanish. Her only slips were a few set phrases that she left floating in the air. Like when she told us she and her mother had decided not to 'come back' to Chile (she meant 'come back *for good*'). Her Spanish was correct but old-fashioned, the kind you might still hear in parts of Sweden, Berlin, Canada, but which to me sounded hollow, or perhaps hollowed out.

My mother asked after Hans: 'Why didn't he come to bury Ingrid?', 'What are you doing here on your own?', 'Why isn't he helping you?', and Paloma explained that her parents had separated, they'd lost contact after the divorce and his remarriage. And then my mother, cutting straight to the chase, leant forwards in her seat and asked: 'And why didn't *you* ever come back to Chile?' (and she, too, meant why hadn't you 'come back *for good*'). Paloma didn't answer and barely said a word for the rest of the meal. She had come to listen, and listen she did, attentively, as she munched her way through the thick artichoke leaves in front of her, taking them one by one, inspecting them, drawing each one to her mouth, sucking delicately on that greyish flesh before putting them back on her plate in a perfect circle. My mother, by contrast, took bunches at a time which she plucked greedily from the heart, glancing sideways at my full plate and telling me between mouthfuls that I'd never finish at that rate ('eat up, Iquela, drink your milk, eat what's been placed in front of you, there are starving people in the world, people suffering, suffering terribly and you so glum, my girl, go on, crack a smile, show me those white teeth of yours').

Paloma topped up her glass and I did the same, fantasising about how we might sneak off again, like that time we'd gone around minesweeping leftover drinks. But my mother had us cornered with her tales of Ingrid and Hans and the day they'd sought *asilo* – asylum – in the embassy. Paloma put down her glass, leant forward and spelt out each letter of *asilo* with a look I hadn't seen before: the look of someone coming to the painful realisation of how little they knew.

My mother used the opportunity to reprimand Paloma for not knowing something so important about Ingrid, 'something so key', she said, and she asked me to explain to Paloma in English what *asilo* meant.

'You translate, don't you, Iquela? Explain *asilo* to her.'

It seemed young Paloma didn't speak such perfect Spanish after all. It was a *key* detail. But 'key' meant one thing for my mother and something else entirely to me: *key* . . . something locked up, something secret. And an asylum was a place with padded walls where they sent crazy people. Paloma's problem wasn't the language, but the weightlessness of that word. That's why I didn't respond, and, faced with my silence, it was Consuelo who finally spoke (because it was Consuelo, not my mother, who would talk about those times: '*her* day'). And I switched off again, trying to avoid falling under the weight of those sentences, convinced, as I had been as a little girl, that we don't live for a set number of years, but rather that we're assigned a set number of words that we can hear over the course of our lives (and some words were light, like 'swing' or 'illusion', and others were heavy, like 'rank', 'scar' and 'tracked'). Each of my mother's words was worth a hundred, a thousand regular ones, and killed me quicker. Perhaps that's why I'd learnt another language: to buy myself more time.

I went to the kitchen for some more water, missing the start of the story. She'd no doubt been telling Paloma about the darkness: about how those days (back in 'her day') were longer and darker. About how she would walk along the streets waiting for the worst, already knowing what would happen. Those were the words that came with my mother: 'waiting' and 'knowing'. As a child I would beg her to tell me this very story, which was full of characters that we knew in real life. I would ask her not to spare any details and she would oblige, telling the story in the present tense with a faraway look in her eyes, travelling back to that place where it had all happened: 'I can still see the wall right in front of my eyes,' she would say. I heard Paloma ask her to start from the beginning, not to skip any parts.

'How did you meet?' she asked, and I shut the kitchen door behind me.

On top of the fridge, the television was still on but with the volume turned down. Grey letters were racing across the screen: CAR BOMB IN MIDDLE EAST. SUDDEN FALL IN DOW JONES. RECORD TEMPERATURES IN CENTRAL CHILE. Two bottles of wine were waiting on the table next to a Chilean salad, not yet tossed, which would go with the second course. My eyes began to water and I decided to pick out the onion – so much more raw, sliced onion than tomato – and boil it to take the edge off. Fragmented sentences filtered in from the other side of the door – obstinate lines, determined to reach me.

'How old were you?' Paloma's voice sounded deeper, or perhaps older now. My mother was talking about the day she and Ingrid met.

'We were so young,' she said, describing in minute detail that emotional, revolutionary, *key* meeting. That's where they'd first laid eyes on each other: on the other side of that black-and-white photo that still hung on the wall. A dog-eared wooden frame with faded edges, and inside, still frozen there, an army of men and women standing before a podium, listening avidly to a speech and all facing the only sign of an escape from this image: a blurred, moving finger. Everything else was static: hundreds of soldierly figures, slogans set in stone and a dead tree in one corner. Maybe Paloma would decide to capture that old photo with her vintage camera, choose a frame, get it into focus and capture it (and I would be left with the remains, with every-thing around the image).

The kettle let out a sigh followed by a shrill whistle, which drowned out the conversation going on in the dining room. I felt my shoulders and neck relax, and left the kettle there on the stove: a deafening screech, a moment's respite in which to think about nothing. But when I turned off the hob all those words came flooding back, uninvited.

In the photo you could make out Ingrid standing at the back of a crowd (although the correct term wasn't 'crowd', but 'faction', 'masses', 'front'). The tips of her fair hair were lightly grazing the collar of her blouse, which looked white, although it might just as well have been yellow or cream. Colours didn't exist in that photograph. There were only differing shades of white, greys that were more or less grey, and a lot of black. She was the only one not looking at the man giving the speech. Felipe's parents – even if my mother refused to acknowledge them, even if she'd do anything to block them out of the story, as if that way she could erase their bodies, and, with it, the pain – seemed particularly dis-ciplined, captured in the final moment of devoted attention. Ingrid's face, by contrast, was gazing in the opposite direc-tion, into the camera; Hans was there, on the other side of the lens, twisting it back and forth, in and out of focus. Hans with Paloma's camera, I suddenly realised. And further back, behind everyone else, wearing those black-framed glasses that chopped his face in two, leaning against the wall and his body still in one piece, there was Rodolfo (or rather, my dad, or Víctor, because he used to be Víctor and my mother Claudia, not Consuelo). That was the only surviving photo from that time, and the only one in which he seemed like a different person. There was something unfamiliar about his expression: the beaming face, the serene, radiant gaze. In that inescapable photo – contemplated at every breakfast and every dinner for years, at every single meal from my childhood – my dad seemed more alive than ever, and yet, at the same time, on the brink of death. It was a photo my mother loved. She loved it as only she could love a photo; in a way that made me at once sad and wildly frustrated.

I filled a jug with water and went back to the dining room. My mother had got to the part about the cell (cells without mitochondria, nuclei or membranes). They had formed a cell in preparation for the struggle, for the dark days they knew were coming (terrible days spent waiting and knowing). And all of a sudden, we'd reached that part in the story: the clandestine days were upon us, and I stood up and left the dining room, my glass brimming with a wine that, this time, wasn't pink, but unmistakably red.

I wandered around the house hoping to find an open door, an escape route. The wine was turning my legs to jelly, and once again I found myself staggering along a hallway. Paloma wanted to know more about the cell. 'Who else was in it?' 'Which faction were you in, Consuelo?' 'How many died during the early days?' 'What exactly happened?' She wanted the details. The truth.

I came to the guest room where Felipe had slept as a boy and which, some time later, had been used by my father (my sick father, the one with all the tubes, syringes, dressings). I stopped in front of the door, and, in spite of my fear (a fear I couldn't understand, because he was already dead, 'your father's dead, Iquela, don't be so silly'), I turned the handle. The darkness escaped from beneath the door and a vinegary smell seeped right into my skin, hit me smack in the middle of my other face, the one that only came out when I was in that house. I had stomached every last drop of that old smell: the fusty stench of illness, the sickly-sweet taste that promised a pain which, for me, never came.

Even from the hallway I could still make out voices in the dining room. My mother's solemn tone told me where the conversation was heading, just in the same way that, in that house, I knew exactly where the floor would creak beneath my feet. Her memory took no shortcuts (disciplined, obedient, militant, that memory of hers). The things she remembered weren't arranged according to the decades or seasons. And hers wasn't like my memory, which fixated on colours and textures. My mother's memory functioned like a topography of her dead, and there it was, laid out before Paloma for her to navigate freely.

I stumbled back to the kitchen and turned up the volume on the TV set. The weatherperson was forecasting another day of infernal heat. The onions were floating limply in the boiling water. I drained them, mixed them with the tomatoes and, now testy and drunk, rejoined the others at the table.

Consuelo had reached the part about the embassy. The part when everyone, apart from her, decided to leave. The part when Hans, Ingrid and my father (Víctor, she meant Víctor) hatched a plan to flee Chile, an idea that she had considered cowardly (she had wanted to fight, to resist). My mother glanced at me when I sat back down.

'You're drunk,' she said, her own lips also stained and cracked. 'I don't like you drinking so much, Iquela. Just sit still and listen. One day you'll be telling your children all my stories and you won't have the first idea. Because these are the stories they'll want to hear, Iquela. *My* stories,' she stressed (and I counted three glasses of wine, nine artichoke leaves and the odd non-existent child).

The plan had been to meet at the corner of the German embassy. At twelve noon, they would all jump the wall and be gone. Paloma knew this hadn't happened, however: only Ingrid and Hans had gone over. That's why she looked up suddenly (her vacant eyes, eyes that hadn't seen enough, distrusted Consuelo). But on my mother went. Now we'd got to the part about the change of guard. A window of opportunity. Four minutes. They'd done their homework, made their calculations. Rodolfo (Víctor, Víctor, Víctor) just had to get there on time. That was all.

In the distance I heard the voices from the television set fade to jingles and then someone introducing a detective series. Paloma's lips were purple and she was sweating profusely, just like me. Soggy onions mounted up on both her and my mother's plates – the terrible synchrony of what gets eaten and what gets left. It was a collusion that left me feeling even more alone: my plate spotless and theirs half-full.

In the end, Rodolfo didn't show. The change of guard finished at noon and there was no time to lose. Ingrid and Hans insisted. 'Come on, the three of us can get over now,' they said, 'it's our only chance.' But my mother couldn't bring herself to leave. She wouldn't jump over to the other side of that wall without Rodolfo. In other words, my mother would stay. Consuelo would resist. She got back into the car and sped off, mounting the kerb. She drove over a row of shrubs and right up to the wall of the embassy, parking millimetres from the building.

I went back into the kitchen, where I listened to the end of the story (the words embalmed at the edges of her mouth).

'With the car parked right next to the wall, Paloma, your parents were able to climb onto the bonnet, then the roof, and from there up and over the wall. They were the only ones who got across. That's what saved them,' my mother said. 'I can still see the wall right in front of my eyes.' (Even I could see it.)

An advert for Mistral pisco came on the television. My mother paused briefly, dividing the story into two neat acts. A pause, followed by one fractious line.

'We stayed behind to keep up the resistance.'

For some reason, the guard change had happened early that day and four civil guards appeared from around the corner in an unmarked car. Rodolfo, on the other hand, didn't show.

'They'd caught up with Rodolfo the night before, but I didn't find that out till later,' said Consuelo (my mother, Consuelo, Claudia, the bottle of pisco on the screen). 'I went underground, but he disappeared for a long time. Eight months with no news, or almost no news. We knew he was still alive because his words left tracks.' (The tracks of people with two names and two surnames.)

I went back into the dining room, but instead of sitting down I announced that I was leaving.

'It's been a long day,' I said, praying no one would ask any more questions. Paloma also stood up and I noticed that her eyes were red. She looked tired and drawn. I gathered my things, and my mother, trailing me like a shadow, looming over me, asked if I wouldn't rather stay the night there. She said it was dangerous out on the streets at that hour. She had a bad feeling about it. I was drunk. There she was again. Waiting. Knowing. It was always the same words of warning whenever I left her house: I might have an accident, I should stay alert, I mustn't trust anyone ('or anything, Iquela, ever').

'People out there are out of their minds. They throw stones now, did you know that, Ique? They go up on flyovers and throw stones down at your windscreen. They'll kill you,' she would say, somewhere between scared and incensed (they can kill you with stones shattering your windscreen, or words that shatter your ears). 'What a way to go. Imagine, after everything.'

Then she would tell me again to keep my wits about me and to call her the second I got in. And I would barely have time to reach the top of the stairs in my building (forty-four steps to be exact) and put the key in the lock before I'd hear the phone ringing on the other side of my front door.

We were all set to leave, my drunkenness and I, when Paloma announced that she was also tired. My mother said no problem, there was a room all made up for her (tubes, syringes, dressings), but Paloma brushed her hand against mine and said decisively that she would go with me, adding that we'd already discussed it in the car. She would sleep at mine that night.

'Take me,' she almost pleaded, and I could only nod, but I also stood there thinking about how that phrase had just opened up a crack in her Spanish. For all the diminutives she'd learnt, for all the swear words she'd picked up, and even for that change of pitch from German to Spanish – higher in the latter – she'd adopted, she had given herself away by speaking so openly and directly. So the euphemisms only came later, it turned out, once you've truly mastered the language.

8

A few glorious months of order and progress, yeah, and all thanks to me knowing how to spot the patterns and make my subtractions, cos even if the mathematicians insist the order doesn't alter the product, everybody knows that just isn't true, cos when I talk about 'the dead', I don't mean any old stiff, there seems to be some kind of order: they find this dead body in Quinta Normal Park, the guy must be about forty, and the next one thirty-nine, then thirty-eight, thirty-seven, like a rocket launch countdown, thirty-six, thirty-five, and on they go dying till they start getting closer to my age, thirty-four, thirty-three, and I've been thinking that any minute now they'll stop, but the corpse this week is thirty-one which means it's really close, too close, and I've still not got a clue what to do about the living dead, what am I supposed to do with them? add or subtract? and when I get down to zero, what then? will some balance be restored? will I be able to start all over again? there's a fault in the formula, yes sir, it's not just a matter of turning up and subtracting them, first you have to work out what to do with the living dead, the ones who are neither here nor there; it's not for nothing that the papers insist on talking about *dead* bodies: DEAD BODY DISCOVERED ON THE CORNER OF VICUÑA MACKENNA AND AVENIDA PORTUGAL, THE

CORPSE HAD ALL ITS FINGERS, they write, as if we cared about the fingers, bah! although, now I come to think of it, it's not such a small detail, because the fragments, the parts, they matter; we need teeth, nails, hairs and fingerprints, but just *finger*prints, mind you, no toes, because the feet are useless, though you never know, I'm going to add my toe-prints to my file just in case, yeah, but none of that's important, not as important as the papers printing a story about a *dead* body, which I might have written off as a slip, but now I think they are trying to make some kind of clarification, to emphasise that there are also *living* bodies, living corpses, the living dead, and that's why the maths gets messed up, because who knows if you're meant to add or subtract, to aggregate or take these ones away, to inter or exhume, man, not even basic arithmetic works properly in the *fertile and chosen province*! but I didn't know that back when I was a kid, when, all of my own accord, I discovered that there was such a thing as the living dead, and I ran to share the news with Iquela, and I told her that I'd seen her dad in the buff and that he was well and truly dead: Rodolfo's dead, I told her, because I saw the bullet still inside him, two in fact, one in the heart and the other behind, right in the back, I swear, I said, because Iquela didn't believe me, she thought I was jealous; she thought I didn't want anyone else to have a dad and that's why she made me swear, so I swore on my dad and on my mum and on electricity and on God and on all the atoms and on the Virgin Mary and on Mary Magdalene and on my marble collection and on my World Cup trading card doubles, cross my heart and hope to die, but I can't really remember if I swore on all of those things, cos those things didn't exist; the living dead, on the other hand, do, and it was Rodolfo who taught me as much,

Rodolfo was in the shower and I needed to pee so I went in anyway, and no sooner had I walked in than I shot back out again, scared witless, and peed all over the door, cos it's not every day you discover someone you know is a living dead, no, but at least I finally understood why Rodolfo seemed sort of gone in the head, like my Gran Elsa, who was also gone in the head, or at least she was going, that's right, she was always going, my sweet gran, until she went; she died and I subtracted her, yes sir, take away one, I wrote in my notebook, or take away half, I should say, cos she was already well on her way, a little part of her had already disappeared, that's what my Gran Elsa would say, that a little chunk of her had died after what happened to my dad, my poor Pipecito, she would say, the only thing they returned to me was his name on a list, and it's true, I saw the list and his name and my surname and then an ID number and the sum of his years, thirty, a number made to be taken away, even though I didn't, I couldn't, because you can't take away what doesn't exist; I subtract bodies, not surnames, though who knows really, maybe someone else subtracted him and I don't remember, me and my damn memory, not like my Gran Elsa the encyclopaedia, it's our duty to remember, she would say before heading off for one of her walks in the countryside, I'm going to clear my head, son, I'll be right back, and each time she would go further and further, so far that it made more sense for me to spend the weekend at Iquela's, because Consuelo can look after you better, it's not my fault, any of this, my gran would say, and one weekend would turn into two, then three, then four and then the whole summer, and all the while she just kept on going, only ever coming back for a night or two, when we would stay just she and I in Chinquihue, she'd come back to warm

my milk before bedtime, to remove the creamy skin that I
so hated, because I don't like things in layers, no, I like things
that are whole, in one part, the full picture, and I can't stand
weird consistencies either, which is why she'd remove the
skin from my milk with a spoon, winding it like pasta before
eating it, yeah, and I'd want to heave and I'd close my eyes
to block it out, to avoid looking at that slimy, snotty gloop,
but I could never close all my eyes, no, the eyes on my skin
were wide open, which is why I'd end up seeing her eat that
skin, and I could never hide my disgust, and she'd tell me
not to be such a fusspot, feral child, she'd say under her
breath, and then she'd ask me if she'd taken her pill, and I
always told her no, you haven't taken it, Gran, because it
was her happy pill and better to be happy than sad, take it,
Gran, take two or three or four, and she would stand up and
look for her pillbox on top of the sink and take a little pill
muttering something about the only problem being that
they made her gain weight, but she was as skinny as a rake,
Granny Elsa; and, in fact, it was one of those times she
mentioned putting on weight that I had the idea for the
hens, cos something was up with the chickens in Chinquihue,
the poor things were anorexic, clucking around in the fields
refusing to eat any corn or crumbs, and my gran didn't know
what to do, because, what with the wasted dog, the depressed
chickens and me, cos I wasn't exactly an angel, and that's
putting it lightly, she was sick to the back teeth, the poor
thing, and it's true that it wasn't her fault she'd wound up
living alone with me, that was that grass's fault, that snitch
who they'd barely had to squeeze before he spilled the lot,
but Iquela doesn't know I know this, and my lips are sealed,
yes sir; the point is, I assumed that the pills that made you
gain weight would a thousand per cent work on the chickens,

so one day I woke up and I knew what I had to do, and I
stole a big handful of pills, I don't know how many exactly,
and I crushed them between two spoons until they became
a powder, and since from dust we were made and to dust
we will return I went out into the yard and called them,
chick, chick chickies, I cried, chick, chick chickies, until
they all came over, and I sprinkled that magic fattening dust
on the dry cobs, that's right, and they seemed to like it cos
they strutted over inquisitively and gobbled it up, and I went
back inside feeling pretty pleased with myself because now
the chickens were going to be plump and happy, but it didn't
work out like that, cos soon they were all falling over each
other as if they were drunk, those poor hens and roosters
were dying of thirst, guzzling water like no one's business
with their yellow peckers, and I was inside, watching from
the window, waiting for them to get fat and happy, but I
soon lost interest and went to my room to play with the
barbies Iquela had given me, Doctor Barbie and Guerrilla
Barbie, pretty, but pretty filthy too, covered in soil, when I
heard a booming cry from my gran, Felipe!, and because,
thankfully, it was rare for her to shout, I shot up and bolted
to the window to see her waiting for me in the yard, tearing
her hair out with both hands, staring at the chickens all stiff
on the ground, dead, really dead-dead, that's what I thought,
though I kept schtum, and she asked, cat got your tongue?,
and it wasn't that, no, because the cats and I were friends
and they'd never try to get my tongue, the issue was that
the pills were meant to make them fat and happy, but instead
we found them conked out on the ground, and I thought
the same was going to happen to my gran and that I was
going to be left alone, more alone than the Lone Ranger,
because she was going to drop dead any day now and that

thought shocked me, it scared me to think she might kick
the bucket and that I'd have to go and look for her like those
stiffs on TV, a missing persons list in one hand and a doleful
look on my face, and that's where we were, both of us silent,
when she stepped forward, crouched down beside Marmaduke
the cock and murmured, he's dead, you've killed him, and
I felt a dagger drive right into my heart, a blade that was
black and hard and cold like those night-time thoughts, and
I sat down on the ground and together we held a vigil for
those stone-dead chickens, as scrawny as ever, the poor
things, and we stayed like that for a good while, neither of
us howling, until something extraordinary happened; at
first I thought I was seeing things, but they really were
moving, in spasms, and after four or five jerks they began
to get up, I'm not sure if any fatter or happier, but definitely
alive, or perhaps alive and dead, living-dead chicks, one by
one getting up as if waking from a nap, and I was ecstatic
but my gran was still fuming and she dragged me by one
arm into the white truck and told me she'd had enough, she
couldn't cope with me any more, feral child, she said, and
she drove for a long time and wouldn't stop to buy me
crunchy *nalcas* in Osorno or blackberry jam from Frutillar,
or to let me have a pee in the Laja Falls, she just drove and
drove all the way to Iquela's, and when we got there she
told Consuelo she needed a break, it was the least she could
do, and Consuelo said nothing and then OK, sure, Elsa should
go home, no problem, she'd promised Rodolfo, she'd promised that grass she would look after me if anything happened
to my gran, and so I stayed in Santiago for who knows how
long until my gran came back for me, and luckily she wasn't
pissed off any more, though she did look pinched and hag-
gard and she had this doleful look on her face, and she told

me that the hens were broody as hell, but not fat or happy, and she was even less so, she was growing scrawnier by the day, you'll fade away, the neighbours in Chinquihue would tell her, and that's exactly what happened, and nobody seemed to care, nobody put a notice in the paper, she disappeared in a flash, the whole and its parts, no stages and no warning, that's how my Gran Elsa died, without a fuss, without a peep, just like my milk these days, thick-skinned.

( )

Something strange was going on and it wasn't the wine or
Paloma or the maddening heat hounding us all the way from
my mother's house to mine. It felt like the calm before the
storm. A rising pressure. But I couldn't be sure. And what
did I know? All I wanted was to escape from that mugginess
and all the words swimming around in my head. I couldn't
forget my mother's final comment, whispered in my ear
as I left.

'Sleep well,' she'd said to Paloma with a pat on the back,
trying to match the frosty greeting she'd been given. Then,
cupping her hand around the back of my neck, pulling my
head in towards hers and hugging me (brushing against
me with her rough, broken skin, her skin that was getting
closer to her bones by the day), she'd whispered: 'I want you
to know that I do all this for you.'

The sweltering air drove me on towards my apartment. Paloma was dragging her suitcase lethargically as
if it weighed a tonne, or as if she were already regretting
not having spent the night at my mother's. I turned back
several times to check she was still with me. There she was,
a metre behind, just far enough for me to pluck up the
courage to ask her about her mother. I wanted to know if
Ingrid, like my dad, had died surrounded by syringes and

dressings. I wanted to know what the chemicals on her skin had smelt like, what her final words had been and in which language she'd died (in as far as there could be a language in which one died). The rumble of the suitcase wheels stopped. Paloma had stopped. On the other side of the street a man emerged from his house and unravelled an enormous tarpaulin, which he then picked up and pulled over his car.

'Always prepare for the worst,' he muttered, arranging the tarp over the bonnet. We moved on and Paloma continued to straggle a couple of metres behind. She would only speak to me from there, as if the story itself predated me and therefore had to be told from a distance.

She told me that she and Ingrid had stopped speaking German when Hans walked out. And so, slowly but surely, listening in to her mother's conversations, those phone calls she would make at odd hours, Paloma gradually began to recognise those silent 'S's in Spanish, and the nouns that shrink things ('*Paloma*', '*Palomita*'; '*mamá*', '*mamita*'; '*cuestión*', '*cuestioncita*'). Slowly she began picking up other words, too, the ones that tripped her up, the ones that meant one thing to her and another to her mother and mine. To all our parents. Because to them a 'cover' wasn't a 'lid' and a 'rat' wasn't a 'rodent'; a 'movement' wasn't an 'action', and 'the front' wasn't the opposite of 'the back'. It was also quite another thing to 'infiltrate', 'fall' or 'squeal', but Paloma knew nothing of that.

She made light-hearted jokes as she told more stories. Of trips to Istanbul, Oslo, Prague. Paloma took photos for a travel magazine. And not just any kind of travel: culinary tourism. She photographed dishes but never tried any of them. Instead, she toyed with the food, rearranging the meat to find an elegant – less grotesque – angle, slathering the whole plate in oil to make it shiny (lustrous dishes, mannequin dishes, totally inedible dishes). Only when Paloma got to the part about Berlin did her tone become a little more serious. She picked up her pace to walk beside me.

Six months between diagnosis and death. She was travelling in Italy when she received an email from her mum. The email's subject: 'theyve found', and the content: 'an abnormal mass in my right breast. love you, m'. Paloma had taken the next flight back to Berlin, going over the email all the way. She could recite it to me by heart. It was written in small letters and the 'm' was for 'mum'. She told me as much when I asked – assuming it was a code name – what the 'm' stood for (and my blunder made me want to scramble even faster from my mother's house).

Paloma had found the subject line – 'theyve found' – strange, and on opening the email two thoughts had crossed her mind. First, that someone from Chile had found her: a member of the family, a friend, one of the pigs, an old comrade (a faction, a cell, a unit), or any number of people from Chile, because Paloma had always suspected her mother was hiding from someone there. Second, and only once she'd read the rest of the email, her mind had pictured a cluster of nuts, and, as she tried to relay this to me, she stumbled over the word 'cluster', so I interrupted her.

'Cluster,' I said, imagining a cluster bomb growing on the edge of her chest. From that cluster of nuts to her death: six months. One failed attempt to remove it (to harvest it, I thought) and three weeks of chemotherapy (to fumigate it, poison it). Ingrid had only been dead five days, but Paloma's account sounded older, like a story that begins 'back then'. Nobody had stayed with Paloma as Ingrid lay dying. She had sat by her mother's side and watched as she stopped breathing, as her heart stopped beating.

'Almost like a pause,' she said.

Not a silent stupor, not a breathless cry; a pause. A simple death. The long list of obligatory calls came later: several numbers were no longer in service (after all, Paloma was dialling numbers from another time), and then, at the back of the little phone book, written in blue ink, she found my mother's name and number, and with them the conviction that Ingrid must be buried in Chile.

'Which cemetery?' I asked to fill the silence. Paloma didn't know yet. She'd made the arrangements for the body to be brought to Chile but still hadn't decided where to bury her, as if another pause had opened up between her mother's death and her burial; as if Paloma had somehow anticipated the trip we would take, our unusual mission.

With her bags packed, all set to leave for the airport to catch her flight to Chile, and with the coffin due to be shipped in a few hours and the particulars settled with my mother, Paloma had felt a sudden urge to repack, this time to include the entire contents of her mother's room: her clothes, each and every one of her books, her slippers, her sheets, her cushions, and the gilet she would wear each night (and which still held her shape, refusing to let go of it); she wanted to travel with all her mother's papers, her towels, to bury her with her computer, cosmetics and creams, to lay her to rest with her tweezers, her records, her cotton buds, paintings and mirrors, reflections and all. Paloma felt an urge to gather together absolutely everything, but the only thing she ended up taking was a faded blouse with shoulder pads. She put the rest in black bags, a tangled heap of clothes to throw out or donate. Finally, she gave the plants a good earth's core. We would play like that for ages, until we grew bored of each other (of our characters), at which point we'd put our own clothes back on, make the bed and unblock the door. Then we would sit on the wool rug, staring into each other's eyes with that sadness that comes at the end of all children's games.

I pushed the door and went in. Sitting barefoot on the armchair, his body bent over to allow him to reach the soles of his feet and paint the pads of his toes with a marker, there was Felipe (and around him a trail of toe prints: Felipe-shaped smudges decorating the walls).

In the background, an irregular buzzing sound was coming from the poorly tuned radio, lending the apartment an air of absurd drama. Felipe looked up and peered at me suspiciously (eyes that saw straight through me). There was something strained about our encounter, as if he'd already guessed Paloma's motives, and mine, as if he already knew about Ingrid's death, as if a predetermined dénouement had been set in motion, although surely it was nothing, or nothing so dramatic, I told myself as I flung my bag at the armchair and surrendered to the final throes of my drunken state. Felipe ducked to avoid my missile and sat taking in Paloma, raising his eyebrows ludicrously high above his eyes, pulling a silly face, playing the joker.

'And who's this?' he asked, flashing his brilliant white teeth. 'A new toy, you sly dog?'

Paloma pretended not to hear him, or perhaps she really didn't. The wine had taken its toll on her, too: I noticed she had the same dry mouth and tired, bloodshot eyes, the same desire for the night to be over. But in fact, without the least intention of taking herself to bed, Paloma went over to the radio, tuned in a station playing Eighties pop and sat down in the chair directly opposite Felipe, surveying the chaos around her: pieces of paper covered in toeprints stuck to the wall, drinks left dotted around the room, the translation error on my computer screen.

'Nice place,' she said over Cyndi Lauper, who was singing away in the background. 'Did you move in recently?' she asked without taking her eyes off a box with DICTIONARIES written across one side: legal dictionaries, medical dictionaries, dictionaries of geography.

I'd been living there a while, sure, but to say I'd 'moved in' was a bit of a stretch. Felipe had bought the apartment with his reparation money ('compensation, expiation,' he'd say with a chuckle) and my slow relocation there had begun with me staying over occasionally, and then gradually moving my things from my mother's house. Leaving without *leaving*. A half-measures move.

The story of my indecisive relocation didn't seem to interest Paloma. Not like the dictionaries, which she got out one by one, flicking through each before dumping them back in their box. She asked if I translated.

'Something like that,' I replied. 'I take on the odd job to earn a little cash.'

I translated foreign advertisements and, if I was lucky, the occasional second-rate script of some shitty, Sunday night movie. Paloma, engrossed in lighting her cigarette, gave a blasé nod before walking up to me and unhooking the camera I'd forgotten was still around my neck. She took a few shots of the apartment but soon abandoned the camera on the table and asked if we had anything to drink. She was exhausted, she said. The time difference had really knocked her out, but she needed to unwind before going to bed.

'Is Consuelo always that intense?' she asked, exhaling a puff of white smoke. Paloma needed to relax, as if she'd heard the line that was still ringing in my head: 'I want you to know that I do all this for you.'

Felipe said we had some pisco and he couldn't think of a better way to round off a night spent in that time capsule of a house than with a delicious nightcap. Paloma removed her shoes and hugged her legs, tucking them beneath her on the armchair. I sat next to her, very close, as close as possible. Felipe served three glasses of pisco and knelt down in front of us, his eyebrows knitted together and his eyes wide open.

'Have your tits grown?' he asked me out of nowhere, gawping at my chest. 'They're bigger, aren't they? Pointier, that's it, like little cones,' he went on, pinching his own nipples.

Paloma looked at my breasts and I snuck a peek at hers: her see-through bra under her white top, her breasts bigger or rounder than mine, less conical.

'I'd love a perky pair like that – much nicer than the German's,' Felipe said, and Paloma burst out laughing and nodded, repeating 'cone tits', 'conical' – memorising the words without taking her eyes off my chest.

I told Felipe to stop fucking around and I tried to change the subject but there was no need. Felipe was already off on one about maths, real and fake numbers and the importance of arithmetic, and I let my mind wander to save me from his neurotic dead people chat – the story of the dismal body he'd found that afternoon, the corpse that, according to him, would change everything.

'Thirty-one, almost the same age as me. Are you listening, Iquela? Don't you get it?'

Paloma was staring at him, either distractedly or indifferently. She flitted between taking photos, commenting on Santiago and answering Felipe's questions, when she would reveal a very different kind of dialect: one she must have picked during her travels in Europe, but which she couldn't distinguish from the Chilean she'd picked up from her mother.

'Let's see now, Fräulein Paloma,' Felipe began, 'what do we call sports shoes?'

And Paloma fell into the trap.

'Sneakers.'

'Trainers,' he corrected her. 'Iquela, where did you pick up this textbook foreigner?'

And Paloma, fighting back the giggles, reeled off a list of words she knew:

'Diaper . . . sidewalk . . . restroom . . .'

And Felipe went on correcting her.

'Nappy, Fräulein, we say nappy and pavement. And don't get me started on restroom . . . it sounds like a place old people go to die.'

Soon everything was making us laugh, and we raised our glasses and drank as Felipe cracked joke after joke – 'This German's one schnitzel short of a picnic,' – and in fits of laughter I translated for Paloma from Chilean Spanish to her Spanish, honing in on the gaping gaps in the language that Paloma was so convinced she spoke to perfection. She was knocking back the pisco. Only her eyes betrayed her exhaustion and drunkenness. We sat there for a long time talking about this and that until, out of nowhere, Felipe asked Paloma what her mother had died from.

'Cancer?' he asked. 'It's all the rage,' and he waited for a reaction that didn't come.

long watering (her mother dead and Paloma watering pot plants, gardens, drenching entire parks).

I opened the main door to the building and directed Paloma to the stairs (exactly forty-four reliable steps). Only once we'd reached my floor, as I looked for the keys in my pockets, in my bag, in my own hands, only then did I notice the light escaping from under the door. I was sure I'd switched it off before leaving. The door was ajar. Nervously, reliving the old feeling of coming home from school to find the white van parked up on the corner, I placed the tips of my fingers against the wood. And just as I used to do with the spare room at home as a girl, I pushed the door hoping to find Felipe sitting on the floor, moaning at me for having taken so long, motioning me to jam something against the door so we could finally play at dressing up. I would enter that room without so much as a hello, and I never bothered to ask him how many days he was staying, fully committed to whatever his visit would offer, to whatever scraps of time he could give me, and I would sit down in front of him for us to call out, in unison, the character the other one was to play.

'Your dad,' I would say.

'Felipe,' Felipe would say, and he wouldn't waste a second in stripping off – jumper, T-shirt, trainers, trousers, even his pants – and then I would undress too and put on his still-warm jumper and his musty socks which smelt of soil and dirt under your nails. Next, standing stark naked, baring his scrawny legs and gangling arms, Felipe would leap onto the bed, whip off the bedclothes and pull them over him, covering his entire body. He played his father and haunted me around the room, wrapped in white sheets. And it fell on me to play Felipe and ask him questions, waiting for his made-up replies: about journeys to the moon and to the

Paloma sunk back into her chair and made a sort of sideways pout with her mouth, a gesture I recognised: she was biting the insides of her cheeks, that slippery, hidden skin. She'd chew until she felt some relief, until she tore the skin away and got rid of that infuriating smoothness, scoring new paths for the cool metal of her tongue barbell, the silvery tip gliding across that raw surface. It wasn't unlike my occasional tic for listing the objects around me, in that it allowed her to zone out of whatever situation she was in. Felipe had shown me the listing trick when he was a boy and didn't want to think about sad things: he'd taught me how to count objects so that they became associated with a perfect, seamless figure.

'The objects turn into digits, which fill the different compartments of your mind,' Felipe would say, 'so that the sad thoughts don't have anywhere to live and we're just left with the numbers. The bad thoughts become homeless,' he'd say, pulling a knowing face, an absent face, a sad, blank face.

I thought about apologising to Paloma for Felipe, but the truth was he was right. My mother regularly called to tell me about this or that friend who had been diagnosed with cancer. That's what she would say, 'they've diagnosed him', as if it were the only diagnosable disease. Bone cells attacking your pancreas, invading your lungs and lymph nodes, distending your uterus, your prostate, your throat. (Bad cells, confused cells, *after everything*.)

'*Habemus* cancer,' Felipe said. 'It'll be our turn next.'

He got up off the floor and began pacing around the room, all the while staring at Paloma, looking for some vital clue.

'So she died in Berlin but you want to bury her here, in Santiago?' he scoffed, his footsteps out of sync with the sugary, pop beat of 'Time After Time', his fingers counting and his face forlorn.

Paloma nodded. Of course, what with Ingrid being Chilean, there was no issue with her being buried in Santiago, but for that she'd had to be returned. 'Be returned,' Paloma said, but I realised that this wasn't what she meant. She was looking for the exact word, but it had escaped her, and I was primed to jump in.

'Repatriated,' I said.

'Repatriated, that's it,' she repeated, relieved and grateful (and I began to wonder if only the dead could be 'repatriated').

Felipe couldn't believe his ears.

'That's all I need,' he said, burying his face in his hands and letting out a pained sigh that slipped entirely from my mind as we moved on to our second or third round of pisco.

He was still pacing around the room muttering and jotting down phrases in a notebook when, eventually, he announced that he was leaving. He was always doing this: upping and leaving without warning. And I always wanted to know where he was going, and why, and how long he'd be. But there was something about Paloma that was stopping him, holding him back. It must have been her eyes, because the only thing she did was stare at us and smoke.

'Cigarette, Iquela?' she asked, inhaling deeply (perhaps remembering, perhaps not).

Felipe eventually came out with the question he really wanted to ask.

'Hey, Fräulein,' he said, already halfway out of the apartment, his hand on the door handle, 'why didn't you just burn her?'

I looked at him agog, certain, now, that Paloma really would lose her cool, and I immediately corrected him as if to protect her from that word: 'burn'.

'The correct term is "cremate", Felipe.'

But Paloma didn't bat an eyelid. Felipe opened the door to go wherever it was he was going, and from there, standing on the threshold, he turned to me and, with a smile, a wink, two chuckles and a shrug of his shoulders, he said:

'Tomaytoe, tomahtoe . . .'

Fifty short steps make a block, but the blocks don't repeat themselves, no, only my steps do: two, four, six recurring steps, and the heat and clouds, and my long drunken strolls, my ambles from Avenida Irarrázaval to Pío Nono Bridge under the starless sky, with only white clouds and a hovering heat, and I let myself be carried by that heat and the pisco, and then, before I know it, I come to the bridge, or it comes to me, the bridge with its dozens of dead, although today it's just one, a thirty-three-year-old corpse, which means I'm up, the arithmetic has to work out because we're heading into extra time, even the newspapers know it, like the culture section today with the headline EXHUMATIONS, yeah, just like that the paper announced Neruda's exhumation, and I would have been none the wiser if it weren't for the newsvendor on the corner, who said good morning and then, well, look who's back from the dead, and for a second I thought about who this living dead man could be, but it was just one of Don José's little jokes because I hadn't been to see him in ages, too busy sorting, repairing, taking away, but Don José saved all the big scoops for me, what is this obsession with digging up the dead? he asked, and I froze and stared at him with all my eyes; disinter, no! surrender, never! I said, but Don José insisted, saying they were planning to order the . . . the . . . and I cried exhumation! thaaat's the one, Felipe, the exhumation of Don Neftalí Reyes, put that in your pipe and smoke it, and I didn't put anything in any pipe but I did buy the paper off him to see for myself, and it's true, they're going around disinterring bodies, bloody hell! isn't that a bit much? first it was the living dead, then came the bodiless dead, and now this, so how's anyone supposed to match the number of dead to the number of graves? how do we make all the bones tally with the lists? how can certain people be born and simply never die? mortuary anarchy in the *fertile and chosen province*! what we need around here is a maths whizz, a numerical mind that knows all about the maths of our end times, because we can't be having all this whereby you die and they give you a real funeral, then a symbolic funeral, then a change of tomb and now what, an anti-interment? it just doesn't work like that! time for some fresh air, Felipe, that's it, take a deep breath, think about the cold and expel all those thoughts, black like petroleum, like grunge, like Mapocho water, cos it's night-time in the river and on the Pío Nono Bridge, two twenty-two says the Law School clock, replace the goddamn battery, arseholes! that clock's always stopped, though who knows, maybe the minute hand isn't the problem, maybe it's me who's stopped, and everything's so dark and the darkness has always made me feel with my skin, this skin that's bristling now cos someone's coming, a pair of pupils in the pitch dark, cos it's night-time on the roof of my mouth and inside my eyelids, just like it's night-time at the bottom of the river, and then I listen carefully and I've not a shadow of a doubt; a voice scrapes its way up a throat to ask me, got a smoke, kid? and I jump back scared because the voice has no body, you can't see bodies in the depths of

71

the night, and despite my fear I reply, sure, but it's not my voice that says it, my head just nods up and down and then I pull a smoke from my pocket and look out east and realise you can't see the mountains, can't see the bodies, no, just some huge storm clouds, white, low-lying clouds carved out of cement, out of marble, out of bone, but I block out all that crap about the clouds and hand him the cigarette, and he asks me if it's my last one and I tell him it is but that it doesn't matter, have it, I say, holding out my hand, which brushes against his fingers, letting me know that this voice does have a body, I mean, it has hands, and they're long and cold and bony, and I hold the lighter up to his mouth and I light it and a new expression emerges, his shining face, his well-defined jet-black eyes, shining puma eyes, a wolf's muzzle and then poof! the night draws its curtain back over his face and the guy thanks me and his voice floats disembodied again, but at least I can see the tip of his cigarette, which he passes to me, and I pop it between my lips only to feel a soggy, squashed filter, but I don't care and I smoke it anyway, and then the guy starts speaking, or his mouth does, and he says Sundays are slow, that's what he says, it's a tough sell but I go out all the same, and I wonder if he means he goes out because he's sad, because it's a sad, shaky voice that's speaking to me now, asking me something I don't quite catch, no, I'm on another planet now because the Mapocho is distracting me, hypnotising me, carrying me away, carrying me far enough to spot a drum, there on one of its banks, a dustbin on fire sinking down to the bottom of the river, and it occurs to me then that those guys must be round there somewhere, the ones the locals talk about, down-and-outs, skeletons dancing on the shore of the blackest of rivers, the dead finding more and more dead floating there, and it's not even Sunday any more on the Mapocho, because two twenty-two means it's Monday, you shitty clock! and as I shout, an icy gust of wind whips my bones and I do up another button on my shirt and wonder if it's those night-time thoughts sending chills through my ribs, that's what I'm thinking when the guy starts talking to me again, he touches me, says I have a nice chest, you wax, kid?, and I shake my head but I don't say anything, I don't want to hear my voice, my voice is starting to grate on me, that's right, I don't want to hear another peep from me so I say nothing, and he carries on talking, saying something about how he depilates all his hair, it's nice all silky smooth, that's what he says, it's nice all silky smooth, kid, and I try to look at him but I can't cos it's pitch black, and he offers me a joint and I say no, I'm alright, that's what I say, despite not saying anything, cos I just nod when my voice goes into hiding, when my voice goes red and burrows down inside me, and the guy lights his joint and his lighter's also red, and for a second I can see the piercing in his left eyebrow and his hair tied in a tight bun, and then the darkness swallows him again, yeah, and I guess I could imagine him with a different face, but the truth is I don't imagine any face at all, because now he's putting the filter to my mouth and telling me to suck, and his fingers brush my lips and he tells me they're nice, you've got nice smooth lips, kid, he says into my ear, his breath all close and warm, and I take a slow deep drag, so deep it hurts, I inhale the smoke into my mouth and I think smoke, fog, blindness, and then I think about the clouds, strangely low, too low, yeah, but I lose my train of thought again when the guy starts talking: I want to give you a kiss, is what he says, and I don't respond and he laughs, and the fire on the shore of the river flickers and the man's voice gets louder then fades and the bridge stops vibrating and falls still, frozen, and I feel a sudden urge to make a noise, to explode, to crunch leaves and crush shells between my fingertips, but I start speaking to him, I've got no other option and the silence is suffocating me, I ask him about dead people, if he knows any or has seen any lying around, and I think I can see the guy staring at me, sizing me up before replying, I don't know that you and I have the same ghosts, kiddo, and then he goes and changes the subject, the idiot, says I've got a silky smooth chest and velvety lips, and I don't care about that, no, cos I want to talk about the dead, not about silky, superficial things, so I ask him if he's ever seen a dead person and he says just once, once he saw a man here, standing on this very railing, just flung himself off and bam! he fell right here, and I ask the man what he did and he says he didn't do anything, and I push for more details about how he feels about it and whether he feels a bit bad, and the guy says, why would I feel bad? and I can hear from his tone of voice that he's shrugging his shoulders, because the voice directs the body, everyone knows that, the body surrenders unquestioningly, and then it occurs to me that the man is right, why should he feel guilty if it wasn't his fault, and his fingers are back, pressed against my lips, and the filter is squashed and soggy and I inhale deeply and the guy follows suit and we cough together and the bridge shakes and I think it's shaking cos there's a seagull on the railing and the seagull is contemplating the riverbed below and that bed is totally still, the Mapocho is silent and without its voice it too disappears, and the guy says it's unusual to see a seagull at night, and I say it's unusual to see a seagull at all, and he asks, how'd you figure that, kid?, and I tell him there's no sea or coast in Santiago and he says it's not unusual, anyone can lose their way; it's normal to feel confused, that's what he says, it's normal to feel confused, kid, and then he moves in closer, yeah, I can feel his breath inside my mouth, you never felt confused?, and I don't answer and the seagull doesn't move and the guy's breath is sour and lingering, and then comes another question altogether, want me to suck you off, kid?, and I'm not sure if I do, but I answer no, cos when I'm not sure about something I say no, that way I can be sure, and he laughs and asks if I'm scared, it doesn't make you a fag, you precious thing, though I *am* a queen, a twink, a bona fide nancy boy, and he laughs louder and comes right up to me, and I'm surprised by the force of his hand between my legs, a slim bony hand that slips down inside my pants and I feel him take my dick out of my trousers, that's right, he takes it out and starts tugging on it and in a second it's gone hard, and I grab hold of the railing thinking that way I can focus on cold things like ice and metal and the river, and his hand keeps moving and my trousers fall down, right down to my knees, and my mouth is dry and my eyes are dry, the river is dry too, and the fire in his hand goes out and the embers rain down on the Mapocho, I watch as they vanish, and I notice that his feet are bare and covered in blood, but I can't be sure cos the hand is moving fast now, touching me, and I can't be sure if there are shards of glass encrusted in his feet, or if those feet are even feet or are they paws, are they toenails or paws? the queen with bloody paws, yeah, and the hand carries on, ah, and I'm not sure, I'm not sure what's at the bottom of the river, I'm not sure why his hand is moving so fast or why it's damp, and I'm confused, I think I see a shadow up there in the clouds, a flock of birds opening and closing like a fist punching the sky, yeah, beating and beating, yeah, don't stop, ah, and the hand moves fast and doesn't stop, ah, and the hand goes on and feels good, yeah, and I come, I die, and the sky caves in and the pieces crash down on top of me, grazing my shoulders, my chest, my hands, and then I lift up those hands and see they're covered in snow, but no, cos snow is white, snow is cold and it melts and this isn't melting, no, this stuff raining down is something else, this is ash, goddamn ash, once again it's raining ash.

(But nothing's blazing. Nothing's collapsing. Nothing's burning.)

( )

When I finally managed to haul myself out of bed all the images from the night before became jumbled in my mind: Felipe closing the front door behind him; Paloma saying she was drunk, that she wanted to sleep, her chest pressed against the window in my room, and her startled voice.

'It looks like it's snowing out there, Iquela. Get up, come and look.' 'Impossible,' I'd muttered from my tangle of sheets, where I'd collapsed from too much booze and too little sleep and was drifting into a delicious slumber.

I got dressed very slowly and wandered into the living room. Despite being half-asleep, I had a strong sense that the city outside had changed. Before the ash came the heat, and with it the sweat and humidity that made everything stick to your skin: clothes, sheets, seats. That heat even found its way into landfills and hospitals, filling the city with a stench of everything stirred together, of a molten us. But now the air in the apartment was dry, a sign that soon we would be back to the usual desert of separate things, things in isolation.

Felipe was draped across an armchair. His especially pale skin, dark bags and the first hint of a stubbly moustache made him look shabby and older. He was listening to music with his eyes closed, bobbing his head along to the drumbeat blasting from his headphones. The skin on his face seemed papery, very similar to my mother's: the texture of it, the muscles and blood somehow retreating towards the bone, made for a striking resemblance.

I didn't want to startle him so I went to the bathroom and used the tap in there for some drinking water. The cold from the tiles soaked into the soles of my feet. My hangover was clawing its way up my head and I had a bitter taste on the roof of my mouth. Undeterred by the closed door and the drums I knew were pounding away in Felipe's ears, I called out to ask where Paloma was. It felt like only seconds ago she was urging me to 'Get up, come and look', but now she'd left. When? And where had the heat gone? It was only then that I noticed the measly dribble of water filling my cupped hands. The lines on my palms disappeared. The water was grey, murky. I closed my eyes. Felipe's voice came back, hoarse with the effort of shouting so I could hear him from the bathroom. I splashed my face with the water. Icy cool.

'Bit of a hitch,' he said. 'So, the phone rings first thing this morning and you'll never guess who it was. Are you listening to me or what, Iquela? Go on, Watson, guess who it was, as laid-back as ever?'

My mother had interrogated Felipe the same way she used to when he was a boy: without waiting for his answers.

'And would you believe it, Ique . . .'

Ingrid hadn't arrived. Paloma's dead mother was out there somewhere, living it up.

I left the bathroom and stood right in front of his chair. Felipe was fiddling with his headphone cable; a black snake wound around his forefinger from the base to the tip of his nail. Consuelo had called at the crack of dawn ('Consuelo,' he said, not 'your mum': perhaps Consuelo picked up the phone and dialled my number from another time, from back then).

'She was upset, seemed in a real state, which is why I didn't wait to wake up Paloma. I had to tell her that her old lady, dead Ingrid, wasn't, it turned out, on her way, that she'd have to ride out her hangover at the consulate.' (The snake all the while suffocating its trapped prey.) 'Can't get into Chile,' he said. 'The country's in isolation. Incommunicado. Interned. A right fucking mess, and you just slept through it like a log, half-dead, even with me shaking you. But don't sweat it, Ique. This is the German's fault, not yours,' he said, unwinding the cable and releasing his choked finger. 'Who told her to bring the whole body here, coffin and all? And on a separate plane. I mean, what was she thinking?'

A sharp pain exploded in my head like an electric shock, timed to perfection with the ringing of the telephone. It would be my mother, or rather Consuelo, who knew the difference. I had to answer it, and then I'd have to schlep the eight and a half blocks to her house, buy the papers, pick her up some food. I'd have to go straight there, where I'd listen to her without really listening, and look at her without really looking, because it was impossible to hold that gaze. I'd be forced to hear her out: I should take extra care, double-lock the door and wrap up against the cold. 'This bitter cold, you're pale, Iquela.' I'd have to nod along, retrace my steps and then do it all over again the next day. After all, she did *all this*, whatever *this* was, for me.

The phone, however, went unanswered. I couldn't bring myself to pick it up (and I counted three dirty glasses in the living room and not one ray of sunshine through the window). I went to the kitchen, turned on the tap and took two aspirin from the cutlery drawer. I opened the tap some more, as far as it would go, the cold and then the hot, but the water refused to run clear. It refused to come out in anything more than a trickle. It seemed to be blocked, clogged up with mud and grime from the drains. The glass finally filled up enough for one sip. Dust and sediment. I put the glass back under the tap and waited. After two more sips I gave up: it was undrinkable. I rooted through the fridge for the dregs of a carton of juice, milk, anything, but there wasn't a drop to drink. Finally, I threw on some shoes and a jumper and I left the flat.

As soon as I set foot in the hallway I noticed my blurry shadow on the floor tiles. I walked down the four flights trying to convince myself that it was just a cloudy day, or already evening perhaps, but the moment I was outside, with both feet planted on the pavement and the weight settling on my shoulders, all other explanations went out the window.

Outside it was raining ash. Once again, Santiago had been stained grey.

With my feet buried in that powder, I stood rooted to the spot and stared at the ash coating the pavement and the news stand at Avenida Chile-España, caked all over the table on the corner of my street where the olive vendor sat trying to work out the correct change from his latest sale. The ash had settled in infinitesimal flakes on the roofs of the cars, in the nooks of wing mirrors and on windscreens, nestled in the hair of pedestrians taking a leisurely walk, their heads appropriately bowed.

I decided to keep walking for a few more blocks. I needed to clear my head, to stretch my legs. The ash had formed a thick carpet that absorbed every sound, and the silence only exacerbated the throbbing pain in my head. I was sure I'd need just a minute to get used to it, three or four blocks to notice some improvement, and, almost unconsciously, I began to feel better. Black and white suited Santiago. The city seemed at home with itself; all those impassive faces and dogs darting about in the ash. My mother would be happy for a couple of days: for once, she and I would see the same thing on the other side of the window. And Felipe, once he made up his mind to actually leave the house, would say the same thing he always did in the ash. 'The cocks will be all over the place in this light. They'll be crowing from dawn till dusk!'

A bus heading to the west of the city stopped on Avenida Irarrázaval, right beside me, and without thinking I got on, ushered by the driver who flapped at me to stop blocking the door. I sat at the back, in the one free seat, next to a woman who was so engrossed in her book she didn't even move her knees aside as I squeezed in next to the window. Outside, a man was sweeping the pavement, spreading the ash around, and an elderly lady was selling broad beans and onion at a table she seemed determined to keep clean, wiping it with the back of her hand.

I followed the woman off the bus at Santa Lucía Hill but soon lost sight of her when her footprints began to merge with everyone else's; there were footsteps leading in all directions, hundreds of identical prints mashing into mine until they became one big mark. There wasn't a single square of untrodden space on the pavement, not a centimetre of ground that hadn't been stepped on, the footprint erased, and then stepped on again. I searched for the woman's face in the crowd, for a fixed point to return to after spinning on the spot, but she had gone.

Still hung-over, I approached a newsvendor and used all my strength to ask him for a bottle of water and if, by chance, he knew where the German consulate was (a grey voice on grey, a trace of calm). The man took his time replying and I glanced at the papers on his stand: 'FIRE DESTROYS POLICE HEADQUARTERS IN BÍO BÍO REGION' . . . 'ANOTHER STEEP INCREASE IN PARLIAMENTARY EXPENSES' . . . 'DRAW IN THE COPA LIBERTADORES' . . .

Only the evening paper, freshly displayed, thought the story newsworthy. In jarring red letters, the headline read 'ONCE AGAIN' above an image, half a page in size, of the Plaza Italia completely coated in ash. It could have been Santiago from another time, a framed, black-and-white photo on the wall, but in fact it was my city, photographed that very morning. Once again.

The consulate was a mere three blocks away according to the newsvendor, who handed me a tepid bottle of water, clearly unimpressed by having been interrupted in the middle of a heated debate about whether or not Cobreloa would be relegated to the second division. I guzzled the water gratefully but it didn't quench my thirst. All around me people were heading to work, calmly going about their business. I headed north, walking at their pace, mingling with the rest of them – with what remained of them – imagining that at any moment I'd bump into Paloma, her head up, scanning the sky for a coffin suspended from the clouds.

I didn't even have to enter the consulate. Paloma was outside talking to Felipe, who was ankle-deep in ash but had not a single footprint around him (shadows leave no shadow). She was shifting her weight from one leg to another, the classic tell of a person waiting for something or someone, but instead of speaking to my face she focused on the wall in front of her (I can still see it now).

'You're pale,' she said, before muttering something else in a mash-up of Spanish and German.

Her nerves had got to her Spanish, which was caught somewhere in her throat, and her teeth were gnawing ruthlessly at her fingernails. Felipe was mimicking this tic, his hand bent in an awkward position, his teeth tearing at the cuticles on his little finger. I wanted to reply that she was the pale one, ashen in fact, but instead I chose to interrogate Felipe.

'How did you get here so fast?' I asked, throwing him a gentle punch that he dodged, jumping back. 'Weren't you literally just at home listening to music?'

'And what about you?' Felipe replied with a smile and raised eyebrows, looking at Paloma, not me. 'I thought you were watering your old dear's garden,' he said (and the sound of the telephone grew louder and louder).

I thought about leaving them and getting on with my day, with my routine, making up some excuse for being late, going over the previous night's meal with my mother, but Paloma pulled a cigarette from her bag and, exhaling a cloud of smoke into the air between us to demarcate clearly her space from mine, she remarked that the ash looked like desiccated hailstones.

Her blasé reaction to the ash threw me, and it occurred to me that perhaps even she knew this wasn't a one-off. I thought about how learning Spanish meant picking up other pieces of information with it: like how, once in a blue moon, the Chilean skies open and it rains in monochrome. Or perhaps she'd barely given a thought to the ash. The matter of having lost her mother's coffin was considerably more pressing than seeing Santiago buried in dust.

We walked away from the building down that grey hill, and Paloma and Felipe, unsure of what to do, began to squabble. They were saying something about where we would spend the night, what the best route was. Watching them prod and shove one other, it was as if they had known each other for years. They were weighing up whether or not to fill in the form, whether it was worth going through the official rigmarole. The civil servant at the consulate had explained to Paloma that she had to follow some procedure or other, some or other normal channel, she had to fill in a form to restart the repatriation process, this time by land: voluntary repatriation of the mortal remains of the deceased (the decedent, the corpse, the cadaver, the carcass, the remains, Ingrid). The lady had explained that it wasn't her problem. It wasn't the embassy's problem either, or Immigration's, or the weatherman's, or the state's. This problem had no name. The flight simply hadn't been able to land before the ash started falling. That's what Paloma was told. Her mother had been redirected to Argentina and was stranded in some far-flung corner of Mendoza.

Ash? again? now that's in poor taste! though, with the city all grimy like this, there'll probably be more bodies, a day of remains, and of remainders of course, our German expatriate, for instance, our lady of Mendoza, what am I meant to do with her? stay focused and subtract her, that's right, a drop of weird rain won't distract me from the task at hand, no sir, I have to work out why the births and burials don't match up; why so many empty niches while the land brims with bodies like one giant cemetery? that's what I'm thinking as I stroll down the Alameda and watch everyone around me in a daze, crazy over a bit of powder, and you never know, maybe it's good shit, maybe if I snort some I'll stop coming out with all this crap, just a pinch, that's all, a bit of ground rock never did hurt anyone, a little line off the back of my hand, yeah, delicious, no wonder everyone's walking round like statues, their thoughts like stone, like the German, who didn't so much as say hello before she started prattling on about Mendoza, as if there weren't enough stiffs here in Santiago, now we're importing them! what a fucking mess, it's anyone's guess if her mum was included on the death register, and if she's included then I should certainly subtract her, but if she's not it means she's been subtracted already so if I do it again, I'll get a negative number, and

how am I meant to reach zero then? by knocking off more
people? exhuming her? and what do I do with the ones who
came back to Chile, after all that time, came back for good?
I could never have imagined so many problems, the maths
is flawed, I knew it, and that's why I was always so bad in
class, always something not quite right about those exam-
ples with apples and pears, let's subtract bodies, sir! let's see
how you solve this little conundrum! but the German isn't
interested in my problems and that's why, when she spotted
me, she fixed those eyes of hers on me, sky-blue eyes like
no other pair in the whole of Santiago, her pupils asking,
how far to Mendoza? and at first I didn't get it, but then I
realised the power in those eyes, as if they'd been born to see
beautiful things and everything ugly faded in her presence,
that's why I thought I'd melt on the spot, because I'm no
Adonis, but she stared at me and I knew why that German
was going to go, because her mum would have wanted to be
buried here, that's what she said, bah, what do I care where
people want to be buried? at least in this respect my mum
was considerate, didn't even trouble us with a funeral, just
dropped dead one day; a cancer of the heart, of woe, and
then, see you later, alligator! and I couldn't even subtract
her because I was a kid and I didn't notice them plant all
that sadness in her heart, all those woes that did away with
my mum, that's what they say happened, and the German
wanting to cross the sierra today, today!, what would a pair
of eyes like those want to cross the Andes chasing a corpse
for? when all she'll see along the way is ash, ash instead of
tulips and candyfloss stalls, but then, light people tend to
see the lighter things in life and Paloma weighs less than a
pack of popcorn, not for nothing did they name her Paloma,
the dove of peace, though really she could just as well have

been Victoria or Liberty or Fraternity, 'Frate' for short, so
creative! it's alright for some, I inherited my name *and* my
surname, like the joke that dies on a second telling, but
Felipe isn't so bad when you consider that I could have come
down the line of Vladimirs, Ernestos or Fidels; the point is
that the German floats above things, even now, walking
through the powdered city, her grief floats above her, yeah,
like the pigeons and the condors and the moths soaring over
the ash, that's what I'm thinking when our German giant
suddenly gets all het up and fixated on the idea of finding
Ingrid, dead Ingrid, and before I know it, it's a done deal!
even Iquela agrees! and I suppose it's true that another dead
person without a body is the last thing I need, and a few days
away never did hurt anyone, what the heck, Fräulein, I'm
in, but you're paying, and don't forget that I'm only coming
out of mathematical curiosity, and the German seems happy,
albeit with a wicked glint in her eye, because the truth is
she's enjoying all this fugitive business, like people who've
never had anything happen to them their whole lives and
then boom!, something incredible happens, it rains ash on
them and they feel like the star of their own movie, not
realising that they're not the star of anything, we're extras,
Fräulein, every one of us, not even bit parts, just look around
you at those faces staring at the ground, look at them, look
at me, but I didn't say that to her, I chose to keep schtum
and let her have her little fantasies, the stories she'd tell her
German friends, about, say, the arse end of nowhere covered
in ash and how her mother was on some rickety old plane
and that's why it couldn't land in Chile and why she set
off for Mendoza, what a Saviour! our heroine! and all those
other German giants will stare at her, their eyes like plates,
and she'll nod along solemnly, with the solemnness of an

orphan she'll nod and lap up the attention, yeah, she'll revel in it as if she were someone important, though who knows, maybe the poor German really is feeling down, her mother has died, after all, and maybe underneath she's upset and she's frightened, cos why play mister tough guy? it is a little frightening, the ash falling so hard, hammering down, thick and fast, over the city.

( )

Felipe was surprisingly quick to agree to the plan, as if his sole ambition in life had always been to recover Ingrid from the other side of the *cordillera*. I, on the other hand, had my misgivings. Or if not misgivings, exactly, I felt unnervingly removed from it all, as if I couldn't even imagine the journey, as if it were a scene from a road movie that I would never play a part in. But Felipe was dead set on going, and even though I was the one who'd always dreamt of travelling, it was he who went places and my job to follow him, to find out for my mother when he'd be back. He wasn't to go out alone. My mother had warned me as much when his Grandma Elsa died and Felipe came to live with us in Santiago. It was an old promise (and the old ones weigh twice as much as the new ones) and Felipe took advantage of it. Incapable of staying put in one place for more than a couple of weeks, he would vanish from the apartment, forcing me to come up with all kinds of stories to cover for him: 'he's in the bathroom, Mother', 'he's sleeping', 'he's lost his voice'.

If I'd had a say in the matter, the three of us wouldn't have gone anywhere, especially not right away. Had it been up to me, I would have drawn the apartment curtains to block out the horrible symmetry of the streets, the cement-coated trees, the children already accustomed to the ash, building castles out of it. I would have told Paloma to be patient. Her mother certainly wasn't in a hurry. But I couldn't persuade her to let me stay behind. 'Two days at most,' she replied when I tried to convince her that I had to be in Santiago and asked her to understand ('*my* mother, Paloma, mine').

Still undecided, I walked for a few more blocks before eventually resolving to go with them, to see the city from above, and then come straight back. I'd ask my mother to lend me her car and we'd take the mountain road.

'Sounds simple enough,' Paloma said as we strolled through Forestal Park, Felipe whistling at the dogs who in turn were barking at a perfectly still Mapocho River. Only once we'd all agreed to the plan did Felipe come out with the real obstacle.

'And where will we put the body?' he asked, freezing on the spot.

'My *mum*,' Paloma corrected him with a little punch on the arm (an unbearable caress). 'My mum, Felipe. Stop referring to her as *the body*.'

But Felipe wouldn't let it drop and walked right up to Paloma.

'Your mother's dead body, Fräulein. Her body,' he said, biting the air a centimetre from her face (and a fine powder settled on their shoulders, making them look hatefully alike).

And there, precisely, was the rub: Ingrid was dead. The image of a coffin tied to the roof of the car seemed reason enough to call the whole thing off, but within barely a couple of blocks, those two had come up with the solution.

The Hogar de Cristo funeral home was just about to close – the steel roller shutters were gliding down to the ground – when Felipe ran ahead, stuck out his foot, bent down and banged on the door until a man dressed in black reluctantly came to attend them. He led us from a dark reception area (eight seats, a screen, a solitary weeping fig) to a room arranged in a maze of identical cubicles with office chairs and ergonomic keyboards. Felipe began talking before even taking a seat. The man listened keenly but soon lost his patience when he realised what our plan was. He pulled away in his chair, stood up and pointed to the door.

'Are you out of your minds?' he asked, brandishing a catalogue of funeral services. 'We don't rent by the hour, sonny. Prices are per service. This isn't a motel, and it isn't Rent-A-Car.'

Felipe and I left the place in stitches. Paloma, on the other hand, was gnawing her nails, red with rage. I tried to calm her down, to touch her, but this only made her walk faster, storming ahead as if we might find another funeral parlour around the corner. Which is, in fact, what happened. In the middle of Avenida Vicuña Mackenna, almost unrecognisable under a blanket of ash, we found a hearse parked up waiting. ('Always prepare for the worst,' the man covering his car the night before had said.) I crossed the street, incredulous. It had to be a mirage. But Felipe was only too happy to dispel my doubts.

'Mercedes Benz, 1979,' he said before striding towards an old, single-storey colonial house, its brickwork cracked from past earthquakes and the windows clad in dark iron bars.

Above the door frame, hanging on a single nail, a sign read, 'Fun al O tega & Ort,' and just beneath, 'Fifty ears with you i your gri f.'

The man who opened the door was young, tall and slim, his face pockmarked by years of adolescent acne. He left us standing on the doorstep while he eyed us up. On seeing Felipe he stood up straight and held out his hand in a robotic gesture.

'I'm deeply sorry for your loss,' he said in a sombre voice while nodding his head.

He was extending his sympathy to Felipe. Not to me, and not to Paloma. The aggrieved party was Felipe, who returned the man's greeting through pursed lips, clearly fighting back the giggles. They stood there like that, as if they didn't know how to snap out of that gesture, those mechanical condolences, and it occurred to me then that they were flirting, that their handshake had gone on longer than was necessary.

It was cold in the house, and as we walked in I heard a man singing along to a cumbia track in the room next door. An intense smell of fried food pervaded the hallway, making my eyes smart and forcing me to take a few steps back to get some air (onions or ash, there was no alternative). My attention turned to a living room with a tall ceiling and five coffins arranged in the middle of it. Cracked and dirty paintings of flowers hung on the walls. Felipe moved in to read the inscription beneath the image of calla lilies.

'We provide traditional wreaths, inside pieces, rose wreaths, teardrop casket sprays and floral pillows,' he read out with a snicker. 'I guess the pillows are to make the stiffs more comfortable?'

Paloma either didn't hear or chose to ignore him. She was staring at the wood of a casket, appreciating it, stroking it with the tips of her fingers as the young man reeled off a list of characteristics from memory.

'Superior, hardy wood,' he said, rocking from side to side like a pendulum by the door.

We were interrupted by a creaking floorboard and the appearance of Ortega Senior, taller than his son but also quite large, with a steady gaze and thick eyebrows weighing down on his eyes. He came over, dragging his slippers and meticulously drying his fat, calloused hands on a tea towel. He gave Ortega Junior a slap on the back (a pointed thump, which put a stop to the latter's swaying) and told him that it was a matter of experience, he must watch and learn how to get it right, before adding that his son had no doubt messed it up again. I didn't understand what he was talking about until he entered the room properly. He looked at us one by one, checking us over, then pinched his eyebrows together into a single line.

'I'm so sorry for your loss, young man,' he said confidently. Next, and in sequence, he took Felipe's hand firmly in his, stroked Paloma's arm, and finally took my hand as if it were a baby bird, nestling it inside his own with heart-rending tenderness. 'My condolences to you both,' he said, his eyes welling up.

We all mumbled thank you in unison.

Ortega Senior listened to Paloma without interrupting her. He nodded as she explained what had happened at the consulate, the forms, the plane diverted to Mendoza.

'I'm German,' she explained. 'I'm just visiting. Help me,' she begged in a sugary voice.

Her story, told without pauses, sounded ludicrous, and I had the distinct sense that I was locked inside a dream. Ortega, however, seemed more than happy to hear her out, and he didn't consider her cause to be hopeless. He only added, with galling solemnity, that he too would want to be buried in his *patria*, that anybody, all of us would want to be buried in our *patria*.

'You've done the right thing,' he told Paloma, and he disappeared for a moment, again dragging his slippers.

94

When he came back he was carrying a set of keys and a cushion under his arm. 'So you can all sit up front,' he said. 'It's bad luck to ride in the back of the General,' and he handed the cushion to Felipe, who was still spellbound by Ortega Junior. He seemed shorter and skinnier now, as if the mere presence of his father had shrunk him.

Together, father and son accompanied us to the door, and, once outside, Ortega Senior handed me the keys and looked at me doubtfully, his eyebrows hanging low over his puffy, bulbous eyes. I thanked him and sat at the wheel. Paloma took the other window seat and Felipe squeezed in between us. It was that simple: we would pay him on our return and call if there were any problems. I wound the window down to get one last look at him and he took the opportunity to repeat, giving the hearse a couple of little dusty pats, that I should drive carefully.

'Careful with the clutch, it's a tricky one. The General is getting on a bit now, although he hasn't failed me yet.' ('Failed,' I thought, pondering that failure.)

The General was cramped inside, or at least the front compartment was, the part reserved for the living. Felipe could barely squeeze his long legs into the space between the two front seats, meaning they thumped against the gearbox no matter what position he sat in. Hanging from the rear-view mirror, a toy Dalmatian and a photo of a young Ortega Junior swung to the rhythm of the vehicle, first watching then turning their backs on us. Only Paloma seemed comfortable, her legs scooped up onto those rough, threadbare seats and her eyes glued to the wing mirror, where five, maybe ten cars had lined up in a tailback, of which we were at the front. They followed us in an orderly fashion with their headlights on.

The moment we set foot back inside my apartment, something felt wrong again. I blamed Paloma, who was adamant that it was a bad idea to tell my mother about our trip (and I counted four round halos where the mugs had been, seven cigarette butts in an ashtray, and the eight and a half blocks to cover). Paloma thought it best for us not to disclose our plans: my mother would only worry.

'She doesn't tend to, how can I put it, take things lightly,' she said, proposing that we only tell her what we'd done afterwards, once we'd come back with her (and by 'her' she meant her dead mother, and by 'what we'd done' she meant repatriate her, if there was such a thing as a *patria* to return to).

I could barely keep up with the conversation. It was only a short trip and she was sure that my mother, too, would want Ingrid to be buried in Santiago. She'd be proud of us for getting her back: it was the kind of thing she would have done (the kind of thing that was *worthwhile*). It's a good idea, I told myself, but I couldn't shake the image of my mother cleaning the magnolia leaves, wiping each blade of grass, removing the dust now settled on the acanthus and paving stones. I pictured her shaking the trees and sweeping the floor, only to sweep it again, and once more. I pictured her dialling my number on repeat, wondering, exasperated, why I wasn't picking up, what was taking me so long, why I'd forgotten about her. I saw her, stubborn as she was, dialling again, her breath misting up the mouthpiece, asking why I hadn't picked up earlier, what I was up to, where I was going, why Mendoza?, for how long? 'For exactly how long, Iquela? Don't lie to me,' she would say. 'What could be so urgent now when all you ever do is waste time?'

So much wasted time.

(Where are you, Iquela? How much longer? Are you on your way? Did you read the paper? I can't understand why you don't buy the paper. The ash. Cover your mouth. All the arsenic, the magnesium, the nitrates, the smog. You're pale, Iquela. You're thin. You're alone, Iquela. So young and so alone, my child. So alone . . . Still such a child.)

( )

I left Santiago without leaving, or without believing that I was really getting out. The ash was coming down even heavier as we made our way out of town and towards the foothills. Behind us, the road disappeared in a cloud of dust. Crouched on the floor to my right, Felipe was humming a vaguely familiar tune, which I soon recognised.

'The wheels on the bus go round and round, round and round . . .'

He had put on his little-boy voice and was reliving the memory of being in the back seat of the car, banging my mother's headrest euphorically ('shush now', 'seatbelt', 'calm down, Felipe'). It was always the same. First he would tell me to sit right back in my seat.

'Let's try something, Ique, let's play hangman,' he would whisper in his little-boy voice, so that only I could hear it. And I would shrug my little-girl shoulders, convinced that he was about to pull out a pencil and pad and that our game would entail guessing the right vowels or burning at the stake. But Felipe never wanted to play *that* hangman; he wanted to play the version he'd invented himself, back in Chinquihue, which is why he would pull out a pencil and a long piece of black thread from his rucksack.

'Stretch out your fingers, Ique. But don't move,' he'd say, splaying my short, stubby fingers.

With my hand resting steadily on his knees, palm facing upwards, on each of my fingertips Felipe would painstakingly draw two black dots for eyes, a circle for a nose and a straight line for the mouth: five mean-looking faces. Then we'd switch roles: now it would be my turn to draw figures on his fingers. I'd give them little ties and curls, and together we'd snicker, wave our hands as if saying goodbye, and tickle one another. And then came 'Eeny, Meeny, Miny, Moe'.

'. . . if he squeals, let him go, Eeny, Meeny, Miny, Moe!'

One of Felipe's fingers – the selected one – would come to the front, and the other fingers would bow in solemn reverence while my hand – my five obedient soldiers – took hold of the thread, the long rope, and tied it firmly.

'Tighter, Ique, tie it tighter,' he would say (his voice revitalised, high-pitched; impossible, that voice).

And I would watch as the blood built up at the tip of his strangled finger, those drawn-on eyes bulging as the thread cut deep into the top joint, a head on the brink of bursting, and our stifled laughter, because we mustn't make a peep, that's what my mother would say, 'Stop that racket, for heaven's sake, there's a special bulletin.' (The drums, the gross persistence of those drums.)

Back in the present, the *cordillera* was looming over us like an apparition. I said something to the others about how dark the sky was, the fields buried under a carpet of ash, the wind's texture now visible somehow: a grey shroud over Santiago. I had to pinch myself to believe that I was really leaving. It's a trip, it's real, I thought, putting my foot down to the max and feeling another flutter in the pit of my stomach. Felipe was engrossed in a pile of newspapers and Paloma had taken charge of the map, as if she'd been planning to rent a funeral car and cross the *cordillera* ever since she was back in Germany.

'Take Route 5 northbound, then Route 57 heading for Río Blanco and Guardia Vieja.'

I followed her instructions until I noticed the incorrect names, the altered distances, the geography of a bygone city (she was directing us out of a city from another time).

We stopped for petrol a couple of kilometres before the border. The pump attendant was killing time, dozing beneath an awning with his legs stretched out and a newspaper for a hat. Felipe got out to buy something at a vending machine (one coin, two coins, he himself an automaton) and the guy leapt up, and gave Felipe a peculiar kind of bow. Once again, the condolences were for him. Then the attendant came over and, giving the hearse the once-over, even peering into the rear window, he enquired about the coffin (the corpse, the sarcophagus, the casket, the house). He didn't seem particularly interested in the answer. He'd spent the whole day on his own and wanted to talk.

'It's dull as hell, imagine. So you guys are headed for the snow, are you? You've never been to the mountains? Seriously? Just go, you'll see. It's really something,' he said and then gazed upwards, hypnotised by those ash-cloaked peaks.

The bends in the road were getting sharper and I regretted having given in to Felipe's pleas. Now I was the one crouched on the cushion and he was behind the wheel. The photo of Ortega Junior was swinging from side to side, as was I, barely managing to keep my balance. The road was one interminable zigzag and my heart was in my mouth as Felipe took each bend without braking.

'Don't you girls slip into a trance now,' he said as we climbed that never-ending corkscrew.

We couldn't laugh. With her right hand Paloma was clutching the door handle. Her left one was resting on my shoulder, either to stop herself from toppling sideways, or to stop me from rolling around on the floor. After a dozen or so bends, she couldn't take any more.

'Let's stop for some air,' she said. 'I feel sick.'

From the roadside, perfectly still, the valley of Santiago stretched out before us, a sunken basin between the mountain peaks with the odd light dotted around. The road we'd just come from showed not a trace of either the hearse or us; the ash was falling so heavily that it was impossible to leave tracks. Paloma was struggling to breathe and had covered her nose with one hand, holding on to my arm affectionately with the other. Or perhaps it was merely to prevent herself from collapsing. If she'd only taken a few deep breaths she might have been able to calm down. Felipe and I had no trouble breathing that thin air. He wandered off in the direction of a cave that had somehow managed to cling on to some snow, even after the heat of the preceding days. He moved swiftly through the ash, just as he used to dash along the beach when we were children, ripping his clothes off despite my mother's cries of 'No, Felipe! Put your clothes back on right this minute. The flag's red, it's not safe!'. Felipe would strip off and run bone naked into the waves, hurling himself at the sea the only way he knew how: like a wild animal. He didn't dive in to swim, but as if to drive his scrawny body into the spray, or rather the waves: to pierce them. I pictured Felipe running – sprinting at lightning speed – across the black pebbly sand of Chinquihue, picking his feet off the ground as he reached the water's edge, taking off. With his legs still in the air his body gradually disappeared into the water, until the inevitable happened; until, from where I stood waiting (from the dry shore, from the obedient shade of the shore), I could no longer see anything but his hands, his fingers breaking the waves that in turn broke him, tossing him into a whirlpool, swallowing him up for fifteen seconds (fifteen seconds exactly, which I counted, terrified), until he emerged again shaking and spitting. He was soon back again, tumbling into the water, slicing through it until, eventually, he came out, numb, breathless and blue, his eyes sore and his teeth chattering, telling me how wonderful, how refreshing the water was.

Felipe approached the cave where the enduring snow held on, completely impervious to the ash, and from there he shouted back that there was still some left. 'Come and see! I've never touched snow before,' he said with his back to us. Then he turned to face us and held out his arms, smiling. His hands were cupping a horrible grey mush, slushy droplets of which were dripping through his fingers.

I pleaded with Felipe for us to get back on the road. It was getting dark and the ash was driving me mad, sticking to my skin. I wanted to make a move before I got stuck there, buried in the stuff. Felipe glared at me, challenging me to put up with fifteen minutes of ash on my shoulders. After some time trying to persuade him I managed to get us all back into the hearse: Felipe annoyed, Paloma indifferent, and I calmer, although my sense of relief was short-lived. The road ahead was a black horizon. Most of the street lights had burnt out and the route to Uspallata had become impassable. We had no choice. Felipe came off the main road and, heading deep into the valley, losing himself there in the middle of the mountains, he stopped the car and turned off the lights.

Night fell for the first time.

I really don't like being stuck indoors, no, what I like is to keep moving, on foot, by bus, or, last but not least, in the General, but never stopping, if I wanted to stop I'd be better off crossing the *cordillera* on the back of a donkey like that poet they just dug up; no sir, I like moving, even more so at night, yeah, cos it's lovely roving around at night, your thoughts all clear in the cold, because our thoughts come out better at night, everyone knows that, the sad thoughts blend in with the black, that's why I take my walks so late at night, in the deepest depths of night, ever since the first time I walked out of Iquela's house, when we were kids and my Gran Elsa left me in Santiago for a few days, just a few days, son, I've some important things to do, she said, and I repeated, im-por-tant, because I liked separating words into their syllables, especially words I didn't understand, or im-por-tant things, yeah, and my gran left, at first for a long time, but in the end for far too long a time, and the house in Santiago began to feel small; in fact I couldn't breathe in there, that's it, I had no oxygen, because back then Rodolfo was still in the sickroom and I couldn't stand his sweet and sour smell, the smell of rotten fruit, of chemicals, which crept right up your nose and down into your belly, and as that smell spread, everything around me began to rot and become sad, that's what I thought, cos in that house even the ficus plants were weeping, which is why I left, the smell was killing me and I didn't want to die, no siree, so I grabbed my things and snuck silently down the hall, crossed the front garden and that was that, but even three or four blocks from the house I couldn't shake that feeling of having sand in my throat, as much as I swallowed and spat it wouldn't go away, no, and I was scared that the smell had infected me and that it would circulate in my bloodstream forever, and that's why I began to pull up flowers, roses at first, which I pressed against my nose to snort up all their scent, sniff them dry, yeah, fistfuls of roses that I used and then threw on the ground before going after the acanthus, with their long white tongues and sweet perfume, so delicious I would suck on them like flutes, and so I went about gorging on nectar as I picked the city flowerless, snatching dismembered petals, petals that I tore from the sepals and the stamens and the corollas and the anthers and the receptacles, which I left floating in the gutters, there among the tadpoles I abandoned those shredded flowers, white canoes in the muddy water for the tadpoles to paddle with, pistils floating with their ugly bug captains, and there I was, winding my way through Santiago munching on the stems and pollen and hanging my thoughts out on the electrical cables to see if they'd light up, like those trainers you often find dangling up there, suspended white planets in the dark sky, that's what I was aiming for, to leave Santiago totally flowerless and to rule over it; I wanted all the pigeons, all the mosquitoes and those long-tailed meadowlarks to be mine, yeah, and I wanted to own the dogs too, to be lord and master of all the stray mutts in Santiago, to be their father and their mother, to open their little mouths, their reeking muzzles offering

me their silvery slobber, the thick, bubbling slobber for me
to store, the rabies from all the mutts dripping into a plastic
bottle, that's what I wanted, and then to put that bottle
against my own wet muzzle, to sniff it and try it and gulp
down every last drop and leave Santiago happy, a calm,
disease-free capital, and I wanted to be lord and master, king
of the mollified mutts, that's what I was thinking as I strolled
along a wide, flowerless street, when suddenly I felt an awful
shiver run through me, the prickle of a bad thought, because
I thought about Iquela rotting in the smell of Rodolfo, I
pictured her sitting alone on the thick woollen Chilota rug
my Gran Elsa had given her, telling me not to go back to the
countryside, she didn't like being left alone with her parents,
telling me to stay, pretty please, and it was this thought that
made me change my mind and go back to her, cos it was no
fun being the king of Santiago with Ique rotting alone back
there, cos we were going to live together, she and I, that's
what we'd promised each other, let's live together for ever
and ever? let's be cousins? I proposed, and she told me no,
I'm going to be your dad, and she drew a black, revolutionary moustache on her top lip and covered herself in the
white sheet that I used to put on, and she handed me the
pinkish dress that she hated, and we played at mummies
and daddies; I was the mummy and she the daddy, of course,
but after a while she stopped liking that game too and I told
her I preferred being her pet, or, better still, her plant, I
wanted to be the pollen, a part of the whorl, because we
were learning the parts of the flowers and I wanted to be a
pistil or a stem or, OK fine, we can be related, but distant
relatives, OK? like great-great-great-grandparents, that's it,
let's be great-great-great-grandparents!, I cried, because each
of us had four grandparents, eight great-grandparents, sixteen

great-great-grandparents and thirty-two great-great-great-grandparents! let's be great-great-great-grandparents!, and she explained that to be great-great-great grandparents we had to have children, and those children had to have children, and they too and then the next lot, but she and I didn't want children, absolutely not, over our dead bodies, how were we supposed to have children when we *were* the children? great-great-great-grandparents, no chance! Ique said, and thank God she did, cos popping out babies would only further complicate things, complicate the maths with more and more tots hell-bent on being born, insisting on being added to the count when what we need is to take people away; babies, no sir!, and so we agreed we wouldn't be relatives, why would you want more family, more blood, anyway? and then she asked me to promise that we'd live together forever, that's what she said, that we'd swear on all the atoms, on my parents and the swallows that we would stick together, and I'd tell her, no, Ique, I can't swear on those things, because those things don't exist, and besides, I had a job to do, I had to look after all the animals and plants in Santiago, that's why I couldn't live at Consuelo and Rodolfo's place, so I told her no, Ique, it's best if we live together-apart, like me and my gran, together but not tied at the hip, and she moaned at me for a while but eventually gave in and swore that there'd always be a place for me at hers, even when we were grown up she'd keep a sofa bed for me; but how could Iquela have me stay with her insides poisoned? that's what I thought as I tried, in vain, to make my way back to the house, because the night was black and my thoughts had got lost, had flown off somewhere far away and were nowhere to be seen, and I was thinking I needed a convertible car, not like the General, no, more like the

Popemobile, to let a bit of air in, yeah, that's what I wanted, Pope but never Pop, that's me! because I wanted to be a lamb of God, to wander around grazing, wrapped in my woolly cloud, and to lie down on the grass there in Chinquihue and drink from the river, that's what I wanted when I was a boy, that was until I saw that bleeding lamb hanging upside down, cos after I saw that I no longer wanted to be a lamb, oh no, but I did want a Popemobile to go and pick up Ique so we could steal flowers together, nibble on parsley roots and loquat shells, but I didn't know how to get back, because my thoughts run away from me at night and I can never seem to steer them back, cos they're as dark as night and they act like those frogs in the jungle, or like stones and ash, camouflaging themselves, that's what dark thoughts in the black night are like, and that's why I couldn't find my way back and I got lost, yeah, cos Santiago was big, like *big* big, and there was no coast to get my bearings, and at that point I did get a little afraid, but just a little, because next thing I came across a stray dog, a pup with a black and white and brown coat, and I could see that he had ringworm and rabies and I thought maybe he could be my brother-pup, cos that mutt with his rabid face walked alongside me, loyal as anything, while I munched on acanthus, and we walked a lot of blocks together he and I, *a lot*, and we peed on street corners and my mutt licked my pee and then day broke and I still hadn't gathered my thoughts, they were still lost in the night and everybody knows that the daytime thoughts and the night-time thoughts never find each other again, no, and I don't know how much time passed, a week maybe, when one day the pigs stopped me while I was drinking from a fountain at La Moneda, the little pup sticking his tongue in the spring and me copying him, just bending over

108

for a sip of water, but the pigs didn't like that and the chubby
one said they would lock me up, and I said, lock me up,
never! I like to roam free!, but he grabbed me by the arm
and threw me into the police van, and there was dried blood
on the floor, thick and dark blood in a puddle that my mutt
lapped right up, and the station was packed with people and
even the cells stank, but not a Rodolfo kind of stench, no,
it was more tangy, the smell of armpits and captives, that's
what I thought, and I looked at the faces through the bars,
eyes brimming with vengeance and pity that made me bow
my head, and there, on the ground, was my pup, literally
shitting himself with fear, his tail tucked between his legs,
his cold little muzzle pressed against my ankles, and the pig
asked me what's your dog called, kid?, and I replied, Augusto
José Ramón and he's got rabies, and the pig looked shocked
and said, you might want to rename him, kid, and I shrugged
my shoulders and he launched into an inventory of questions
like what was my surname, my ID number, my date of birth
and address, and I told him I lived in the gutters with the
mutilated petals and the tadpoles, in the corollas of flowers,
between the sweet yellow suns of the acacia, and he stared
at me and asked, when was the last time you ate, you stupid
prick?, and I thought, who does this guy think he is? I'm the
king of Santiago and the acanthus, but I didn't say any of
that, I just replied with my name, Felipe Arrabal, and he
wrote it down really slowly, as if he were learning the alphabet, all in big letters, big like the German, and I really don't
like capital letters, or capital cities or capital punishments,
but I didn't tell him that because he picked up the phone
and rang the sergeant and repeated my name down the line,
affirmative, Sergeant, Arrabal with Bravo, and I just sat there
while he thumbed through files and forms with a clueless

look on his face, scrunching up his forehead like a bulldog, the spitting image of Don Francisco, and then he hung up and said, impossible, and then in a gruff, angry voice, I wasn't born yesterday, sunshine, don't mess me about, what's your name? to which I replied, Arrabal with B for Bear, for Beast, for Bigmouth, with B for Brute, I said, Arrrrrrrabal, and he looked me up and down with a big frown drawn across his brow, his face deformed and his mouth moving like a dog's but without the drool, well that's just not possible, so tell me your real name or I'll knock it out of you, you little shit, I'll bang you up in that cell where no one's getting you out, and I repeated, Felipe Arrabal, my name is Felipe Arrabal, and there was Augusto José Ramón slobbering all over my shoes, and the smell of lonely people, and the pig's booming voice, his red voice coming from his red face, which was bursting as he said, Felipe Arrabal is presumed dead, and I said nothing, and there were the pistils and the petals and the calyx and the drool bubbling away in the bottle of rabies, and there I was swallowing down the sand in my throat, eking out my quiet reply, whispering the words so I didn't lose them there in that prison, so they didn't turn grey and blend into all that metal; there I was, speaking slowly, looking him in the eyes, feeling the rabies-sodden muzzle against my ankles, and I said, to myself, which is how I used to say all the really important things, I said, pre-*sum*-ed-dead, and I shot out of there so fast they didn't see me for dust.

( )

We decided to park up and try to get some sleep down in a valley, where the night had engulfed every last trace of ash. I could only make out a few sounds: the whistle of the wind, Felipe's fitful breathing and the crackle of the crisp packet he'd bought at the petrol station, the contents of which Paloma was shovelling casually into her mouth. I waited, convinced I'd soon adjust to the darkness, but after a while I rubbed my eyes to force them into focus: there was the photo of Ortega Junior hanging from the rear-view mirror, and that day's newspaper crumpled at my feet (ONCE AGAIN, it read, ONCE AGAIN). Paloma was now holding the map, drawing it in towards her nose and then back out again. Getting nowhere, she finally took out her lighter to shine over the page.

'Los Penitentes,' she said, before letting the flame go out. 'I think we're in Los Penitentes.' (The penitent, the mournful, the grief-stricken.)

I explained that Los Penitentes was a valley beyond Cristo Redentor, crossing the Paso Los Libertadores, whereas we were on an unknown high plain, stuck in the middle of nowhere. Paloma unfolded the map and passed it to me, determined to prove we'd chosen to spend the night in Los Penitentes, that this was some kind of omen, but she could no longer find the valley on the map. Felipe was sitting silently in his seat, steeling himself for the long night ahead, the mere thought of which was probably driving him crazy. I realised that it was my turn to convince them. It made no sense for us to spend hours cooped up in the front compartment, wide awake, staring out at the nothingness, so I suggested we all climb into the back.

'We'll be way more comfortable,' I said, 'don't be so superstitious.'

Ortega's ominous caution didn't bother me; not after the ash, the lost corpse, and now Felipe's increasingly agonised sighs.

So we clambered into the back compartment, Paloma acquiescent and Felipe bordering on autistic. For my part, I was quite enjoying myself. We settled down in a sort of semicircle, trying out different positions and doing our best to avoid the two parallel rails running across the floor (a coffin-gliding device). I found it roomy back there, and I was pleasantly surprised by the silky soft floor: a velveteen or even velvet lining. In the middle of the ceiling I could just make out a small light fitting (the strange urge to illuminate coffins). Just as my eyes were beginning to make sense of the interior layout, Felipe switched on the light to reveal a rear window, a dark sheet of glass separating us from the front compartment and the telling absence of windows down the sides of the hearse.

There were barely a few centimetres separating us from one another, and the solitary landscape, the isolation and the darkness supplied the perfect conditions for a kind of forced intimacy, a confessional intimacy. Paloma couldn't contain herself any longer.

'We're still so far away,' she said, 'and what if the engine gets clogged with ash? And what if we don't get to Mendoza? Where will I look for her then?' And she cracked her knuckles one after the other (ten wasted seconds).

Her fear caught me by surprise, and I turned away and stared out of the rear window. The ash was still coming down, now illuminated by the light inside the hearse. And certainly the night was unfolding before our eyes, but the nightmare scenario of actually getting stuck there seemed unlikely to me.

'It's not such a big deal,' I told her, stroking her leg, which was so cold it took me aback. 'It's only ash, Paloma. It'll soon stop,' and I left my hand on her thigh, not quite knowing how it had got there.

Felipe shuffled back suddenly, forcing Paloma to move to the side, and whipped open his rucksack. Three glasses and a bottle appeared as if from a magician's hat. Felipe served the drinks – his measure bigger than ours – and we immediately took him up on his offer: the sheer pleasure of a neat pisco.

It was my idea to play the categories game. I suggested we turn off the light and lie down on the floor, face up, Paloma sandwiched between us.

'To keep our mind off things,' I said, emboldened by the pisco. 'Why not?'

Categories with no pens, no paper and in the pitch black.

We each came up with one category. I proposed Volcano Names. Paloma suggested Cemeteries in Chile. Felipe initially refused, but, having thought it over for a moment, came up with the category: Ways of Killing or Dying. Paloma took off her shoes and nestled in between us with her legs stretched out and her right shoulder grazing mine. One of the metal rails separated us, digging into my arm and leg. The cold of that steel didn't bother me for long, however, and soon the only things I felt were the letters for our game drawn on the floor, the velvet rubbed against the grain, where I encountered Paloma's hand. I placed my own on top of it and left it there, as still as a statue.

'I'll start,' Felipe said. 'A,' and he ran through the alphabet in his head until I stopped him.

'Stop,' I said.

'G.'

'General Cemetery.'

'Gassed.'

'Gonorrhoea.'

'*Güelén.*'

We threw out letters and called out our answers, trying to one up each other.

'*Huelén* is a hill, Paloma, not a volcano. And besides, you spell it with an H. H for *huaina*, for hacked, for hollowed out.'

'No one ever died from being hollowed out.'

'Oh, but from being hacked they did?'

'OK, fine . . . Stop.'

'M.'

'Metropolitano.'

'Maipo.'

'Murdered.'

'So you can die of murder, Felipe? No way.'

'Of course you can!'

'Mm . . . OK, next.'

Paloma kept laughing at random moments, clearly playing some alternative game of Scattergories in her interloping German. Every now and then she came out with a German word, which she would then translate into a Spanish word that never began with the letter we were on. With every mistake, she squeezed my hand.

'Stop.'

'P.'

'Lots of cemeteries begin with Park,' she said. 'It's true, not even the cemeteries call themselves cemeteries.'

'Peteroa.'

'Puyehue.'

'Puntiagudo.'

'Pecked.'

'Pecked? Jesus, Fräulein! Who was ever pecked to death?'

'Stop.'

'T. T for tent. T for twat. For Tacora. For Tutupaca. For torture.'

Sometimes I repeated back Paloma's German, sounds that caught in my throat and were lost on me but for their friction. Maybe I was trying to gain a little time by repeating the words back to her, and perhaps it was the chafing feeling that seduced me. Because with each syllable spoken in German Paloma's fingers would rub against my hand, a repetitive and painless back and forth which brought back another memory: the memory of my skin hurting; of another time when I used to go through this same ritual. A very shy little girl had shown me her secret. Camila, she was called, and we were classmates for just one winter, long enough for her to teach me the scratching game. Like a drop of water dripping steadily on your head, her finger would move to a constant beat. She scratched. My skin came apart. She and I could spend hours doing it: my hand still and hers moving from side to side, over and over until there was no more space left under her nail, because it would be packed with my flayed skin and congealed blood. And the nail would keep moving, 'faster, Camila, go on', every sound another layer of my skin, 'go on', gaping pink, red, white, 'harder, don't stop'. My hand would take weeks to heal, but at least it offered a real kind of pain: a pain that was visible and mine. And when the first signs of a scab began to show and the wound threatened to heal over, we would start all over again. My left hand still carried a trace of that scar and Paloma was stroking it without even realising.

I tried to bring my mind back to our game, but I was trapped in that old memory (the gaping wound an escape hatch). Paloma seemed to be having fun and, now a little tipsy, she was repeating tongue-twisters.

'Red lorry, yellow lorry . . . Betty Botter bought some butter but she said the butter's bitter . . . How much wood would a woodchuck chuck if a woodchuck could chuck wood? . . . Peter Piper picked a peck of pickled peppers . . .'

Her tongue couldn't quite find its way around the words. Felipe, though, didn't correct her. He was lying face up, gnawing away at his fingernails, driven half mad by the darkness and claustrophobia, so I had to be the one to shake him, drag him in towards me, propose some other game that might protect him from himself. Just like when we were kids and, crouched on the woollen rug, he would propose we play pin the tail on the donkey.

'It's really fun, Ique. Go on, please, rub my eyes. Hold your finger on my sclera for as long as you can.'

Felipe insisted on playing this game, where I was to put my finger in my mouth and then, with the same finger, the tail, touch the white of his eye, the donkey. According to him, his eyelid was the enemy.

'We have to fight against the curtain that wants to come down on us, Ique. It wants to block us out, to board us up forever.'

And so, ever obedient, I would suck my forefinger and tell him to lie back on my lap with his head on my thighs and open that white eye nice and wide for me.

'Go,' he would say when he was ready, 'touch it, Ique,' and I would hold the very tip of my finger against his slippery socket, gingerly stroking that wet surface, first to one side, then the other, until his eyelid could take no more and began to quiver, his whole eye flooded with red labyrinth patterns, spiderwebs that wove themselves beneath my finger.

'Let's keep going, Ique. The other eye, Ique, the eye inside.'

In the back of the hearse, Felipe still hadn't said a word and was struggling to breathe, as if he might forget to inhale and it were my role to remind him.

'And again, Felipe, take a deep breath in.'

Our game fizzled out. Felipe's silence was unnerving me, it's true, but it also presented the perfect opportunity for me to ask Paloma about Berlin, about the names of the trees and parks there, anything so long as Felipe didn't interrupt with one of his endless diatribes. I began with a question about her photography and trips: the typical conversation of two people who have nothing in common. What could we talk about? What could we ask each other? I barely remember her answers. I know she rolled out the names of some cities and different foods, a long list that did nothing to temper the coldness I felt when she stopped talking and a long silence fell, which I didn't know how to break.

'And your dad?' Paloma came to the rescue.

I'm not sure if she was really interested or if she just thought it was the proper thing to ask, like two people exchanging hellos, jackets or dead parents. Whether it was courtesy, my increasingly drunken state, or perhaps just relief that someone had filled the silence, I told her the short version first; the haiku version, as Felipe had once called it when he tried to protect me from my schoolmates' interrogations. They wanted a heroic, bloody story and Felipe was an expert.

'Tell them you don't have a dad and be done with it, Iquela. Kill it with drama.' But they wouldn't leave me in peace. That's why we invented the haiku version.

'He died of cancer. It was winter in Chile. Soon after you came,' I blurted out to Paloma, as if ripping off a plaster.

I bunked off from school for weeks after we buried him. It was Felipe's idea. He'd wait for me half a block along from the gates and we'd go wandering the streets, getting lost. His Grandma Elsa had left him with us that month, but he refused to come to class. We'd walk around following stray dogs, washing them in the public fountains, whiling away the time. Only when darkness fell, after hours of drifting, would we go home, exhausted, and anxiously await the cross-examination that never came. It was midwinter and by all accounts the Santiago cold should have soaked right through to our bones, but I remember not feeling a thing: no hunger, no cold, no grief. After all, my father had already died once before.

'They lined me up and shot me in Chena,' he would tell us in the elevated tone he reserved for that line.

A special voice for a special line. A voice born to speak those nine words. Then he would lift his shirt up to his neck and proudly show off the scar that ran from his chest right round to his back, my mother watching from the dining-room door, her eyes glazed before that erect statue in the middle of the house. With time I learnt to tell other stories. I invented suicide attempts, gory accidents, memorable deaths, just to see what reactions I could provoke in others, to see the pain in their eyes, to try to retain it, copy it, and, later on, repeat it.

Felipe hadn't uttered a word and Paloma joined him in this pact of silence. We'd already covered dead fathers, dead mothers, climate disasters, and I was on my sixth or seventh chewed fingernail when I couldn't bear it any longer.

'Why didn't your mum ever come back. I mean, come back for good, from exile?' I asked, already regretting the question as Felipe let out a snickering yawn.

My own voice sounded brusque (another voice was prising open my mouth: 'go faster, don't stop'). My indiscreet question, which would no doubt lead to a *key* answer, was straight out of my mother's book. But my mother couldn't hear me now. She would be at home, still staring at those black-and-white photos, sweeping death from the door each morning (the telephone ringing for days). Felipe grunted and turned to face me.

'Give it a rest, Iquela. You're such a bloody bore,' he said, blowing his boozy breath into my face and switching on the light above us (his eyes blind with rage). 'What the hell does it matter why the woman didn't come back to Chile? That's seriously your chat-up line for our German friend?'

He almost spat his words out, breaking an old promise that in truth he'd already broken. He'd deserted me, left me on my own with everything (with the weight of all that past).

Paloma sat up, served us some more pisco and suggested we both calm down; it wasn't a big deal. She sounded calm herself, as if two days with me were enough to work out that I'd never get into a full-blown argument with Felipe.

She breezily handed us each a cup. She was enjoying herself. There was a hint of condescension in her eyes, that unbearable neutrality of the mediator.

'Let's toast,' she said, raising a solitary cup, leaving it in haughty suspension. 'In German we say prost. That's it, prost! Guys, it doesn't matter.'

But Paloma had no idea what Felipe and I were really arguing about; or that it 'mattered' so much more in her presence.

'Give me a break, Felipe. You can talk,' I shot back.

I told him it was pitiful watching him with his little notebooks. I said Paloma couldn't be overly happy about *him* prattling on about death the whole time and that maybe he should go and stretch his legs (take a long walk with his eyes closed, out into the night where it made no difference if they were open or closed). Felipe didn't even reply. He just opened the rear door and got out, laughing a hollow cackle, as if in an empty theatre.

Paloma changed the subject and began telling me the story of her mother in exactly the same way she'd devoured her artichoke leaves: methodically, routinely. I barely followed what she was saying. Felipe's sudden outburst, his pain, my rage, my mother at home drenching the plants and all the forced questions (weren't there other questions we had to ask? did it really rain ash during my childhood?) made me feel more alone than ever. Paloma's forefingers were running up and down my arm but I only noticed it once it had begun to annoy me, once her touch became irritating.

'Relax,' she said.

Paloma got onto her knees, moved her face up to the rear window and, taking my hand, drew me in closer. On the other side of the glass, with our faces pressed against it, we saw an inky flatland, and beyond it, moving away from us in a swaying motion, a minuscule red dot: the tip of Felipe's burning cigarette. Paloma wanted to know why Felipe was like that. 'Like that,' she said, and I was at a loss what to reply. 'What do you mean by *that*?' I asked.

'It doesn't matter,' she said.

And she was right: it didn't matter. Not that night, not in the long silence that opened up between us which, this time, I didn't attempt to fill. I moved in towards her and placed my hand on the back of her neck (stroking the body back to front: the inside of the eyelids, the cornea, the creases in the skin). I held my fingers still, nervously, until I noticed her pulse racing under her skin, which was stippled with beads of sweat. I didn't move my hand away, looking for her in the reflection of the window (and her irises dyed the valley blue: the sky turned blue again and disappeared in a blink). Paloma turned towards me, bringing her face close to mine before swiftly pulling away and groping around on the floor about me, lightly grazing my leg as she found one of the plastic cups. She brought it to her lips, tipped back her head and, having drunk the last drop of pisco, raised her arm and turned off the light.

Lying back on the floor, she told me to come and join her. Her voice sounded sweet but aloof: it was too formal, that 'lie down next to me, Iquela, let's get some sleep'. But then another order, in another, more playful, tone, chased away my disappointment.

'Undress,' she said (one booze-soaked word). I didn't take long to respond, but in the brief lull between her order and my reaction, in the couple of seconds in which I thought I'd misheard her, thought it impossible, in which I waited for her to give me another sign or undress me herself, my mind was flooded with dozens of other orders ('come here', 'be quiet', 'don't forget', 'sit down', 'let it out'). I lay down on my side maintaining a space – barely a rail's width – between us, and I inched my face towards hers.

'You first,' I heard myself say. 'You undress.'

4

Cos I'm a chump, cos I'm a soft-hearted schmuck, girls always get their way with me, that blue-eyed German says jump and I say how high and end up in a hearse in the middle of an ash storm, cos that's all I needed, and with Iquela being all bolshie, telling *me* that *I'm* being a pain, me!, now that's rich considering I'm the one giving up my precious time, time that could have been spent on numbers, yeah, cos the dead keep coming and I've got more work to do than ever, and it's impossible to do my subtractions in this darkness, and yet they must be done, the bodies have to be found and they have to be taken away, but with everything so black it's not easy, I can only just make out the line of the mountains, the *cordillera* that looks like a body reclining on its side, stretching all the way down Chile, from north to south, that's the *cordillera*, its big head up there in Arica and its bum down here, and they wonder why Santiago stinks of shit, but, well, you do the best with the hand you're dealt and I was dealt what they call the Intermediate Depression, there's just no escaping it in the *fertile and chosen province*! and I've got no choice but to walk around and plan dead Ingrid's rescue mission, cos it looks like I'm the only one who gives a damn, the German seems happy enough fluttering her eyelashes, and look at where it's led me, coming here to play chaperone to those two, though thinking about it, this trip is the most patriotic thing I've ever done, I mean, what could be nobler than a mother-daughter reunion? only a father-son reunion, cos it's a national tradition, yeah, going missing! and the mysterious case of Lieutenant Bello was a historical milestone: viva the family reunion!, which is why, come Saturday, people like to settle down in front of the telly for the show; my Gran Elsa was always first in line, every Saturday she'd have tea watching the host, Don Francisco, and I would sit spying on her for hours, till six o'clock when the talent show was over and the sad music would begin, that melodramatic theme tune getting louder and louder, and Don Francisco's voice would grow very deep, and he would speak slowly, pulling a face like a depressed bulldog and say: ladies and gentlemen, I'm going to tell you a sad story . . . the story of a mother who has been looking for her son for fifteen years, and Don Francisco would look straight into the camera and a lady in a floral skirt with an apron around her waist would appear, with a head of cork-screw curls and lips on the verge of a weepy pout, and her hands would be buried deep in her apron as she looked at Don Francisco and at the camera, not knowing what to do, where to put her eyes, and Don Francisco would say, Señora Juanita, tell us, when was the last time you saw your son Andrés? and Señora Juanita would mutter her story gingerly and my Gran Elsa would listen, weeping, and the whole of Chile would be weeping too, cos anyone who tells you he didn't watch the family reunions is a liar, that show was the reason I started going out looking for other people's dead, cos I was brought up on Don Francisco telling Señora Juanita, we've got good news for you, my dear, your son . . . your son . . . and ta-da! there would be none other than Andrés, right there in the Channel 13 studio, and everyone would get very excited and the old girl wouldn't be able to take any more, and her pout would now be firmly imprinted on my gran's face as she wept and wept, and it's these kinds of things that turned me so soppy, cos we all like to see families reunited, yeah, and right now no two people could be happier to be reunited than Iquela and the German, that's one seriously good reunion, Jesus! hands all over each other, both well up for it, easing their pain with kisses, and of course, the blue-eyed German knew exactly what she was up to, she was no fool, she didn't hang around, there are ways and there are *ways* of working through grief! shame you can only make out their silhouettes on the other side of the glass, cos I'd recognise Iquela's silhouette anywhere, and there was a time she didn't find me such a drag: I was on the pavement playing chase the hose with Consuelo, though, come to think of it, Consuelo was just watering the plants and I was running through the water, running till she said something, running under that steady stream, but she never said anything to me, only that one time when I'd just showed up at their house from the south, just one instruction she gave me while she set up the pull-out bed in the guest room, you'll sleep here, she said, and I got into that bed she never put away, cos the guest in the guest room was always me and I would sleep each night on my pull-out bed imagining I was a parrot like Evaristo, a little green parrot sleeping in his little house, and I'd still be wide awake come night and that's when I'd hear their voices, Consuelo fighting with Rodolfo, how long's he staying?, he would ask, I remember it all, every last detail, he's the spitting image of Felipe Senior, Rodolfo would say, the only thing missing is the moustache, but that only happened some nights, and the rest of the time they'd watch TV till dawn, or fuck, yeah, some high-pitched squeals coming from Consuelo followed by the living-dead man's death rattle, but the point is that one day back then I was out on the pavement playing with the hose when Ique showed up and we started messing about, she took the hose off Consuelo and began spraying jets of water at me, and I loved it, of course, because it hurt and I imagined I was a weeping willow, she watered me and I crouched down and Iquela came beside me and told me to get on my knees, and then she came right up close and flung her hair over my head and her long locks fell like curtains, and for me it was nice to have long hair and I imagined it was mine and I closed my eyes thinking how, together, we formed a single weeping willow, and we were messing around like this, playing at botanists, at standing in the rain, at hairdressers, when she pulled away from me, came over all sad and said, look what happened to me, Felipe, look at this, and she raised her arms high in the air and showed me some little black hairs in her armpit and then she said, look, look down here, and she took down her pants and with my own eyes I saw hairs there, and I pulled my shorts down and I showed her my downstairs and we touched each other for a while, and Consuelo watched us from the house, and in fact I don't really know what happened next, I guess we just got bored, but that night, when I went to bed, Consuelo came into the spare room and she said, Ique's room is off limits, kid; as if I'd even want to sleep with Ique when she and I had agreed we'd be great-great-great-grandparents, or that she would be my dad and I her daughter, but boyfriend and girlfriend never, no way! we hadn't even wanted to carry on touching each other, cos as kids we weren't even curious about physiology, we were born with the wonder lobe missing, not even the ash took us by surprise . . . well, maybe a little, the point is I know Ique so well I'd recognise her silhouette anywhere, but not the German's, and that German is trouble, because she's climbing on top with no top or bra on, and her breasts are white, that's what I imagine though I can't see a thing, because my breath misting up the window is black and I can't see any more than their outlines, the contours of those enveloping bodies, a pair of orphan kittens who recognise each other, come in for a mutual lick, and their skin is smooth and it's nice all silky smooth, yeah, and what's smoother than their skin coming together and Ique putting her hands in her mouth, her wet fingers touching the German's breasts, moving down and taking her by the hips, moving down and slipping them inside, yeah, and you can tell that the German likes it, and I do too, cos it's turning me on even though Iquela is like my sister, my great-great-great-grandmother, like my dad, I'm turned on cos they're animal bodies, bodies passing each other heat because they're lonely, that's what I think, and then in my head I see my little brother-pup and the weeping willows and the water lashing my back, and I think about the living-dead man's death rattle and the green feathers on my desk, so silky smooth, yeah, and then I feel a burning between my legs, the fire climbs up and feels tight, the heat intensifies and I push it away and the ash is falling and I push it away and the memories come flooding back and I push them away too, and I think that I could just let go, let it all out and then leave, but no, I don't, cos if I did that I'd get lost and I've already got enough missing people on my hands; I'm never going missing, never ever.

( )

It took me a while to sit up, but the vibrations on the floor helped bring me around, back to my naked body, to the plastic cups littered around the hearse and an annoying noise at the back of my head.

'Iquela.'

Open eyes, a grey ceiling and the sound of knuckles being cracked. 'Wake up, Iquela, we've left Chile,' Paloma was saying, having appeared suddenly from behind a pane of glass that only moments ago hadn't existed.

I sat up, avoiding the rails, put on my jumper and turned to face forward. The road was a grey scar between the mountains. Felipe, perfectly mute, was pushing the engine to its limit. I could only see part of his face in the rear-view mirror: one bulging bag under his eye, a single eyebrow, the faintest trace of a moustache, which disappeared as the hearse entered an enormous warehouse.

The border was simply this, a huge, dingy warehouse, though it easily could have been something else: an impassable checkpoint, a barbed wire fence, thumbprints on a page. Or even a sky-high wall (a vast *cordillera*) that would prevent us from crossing in one piece, that would force us to leave parts of ourselves behind. The posters warned us not to carry raw food across and I would have to give up certain words too, leave them behind.

But that is only what the border could have been. In reality, the official state line was marked by a rudimentary, derelict warehouse. Felipe stopped the car so I could climb up front and sit between them on the cushion.

'Got your little tantrum out of your system yet?' Felipe asked. 'Looked like you two had a good time last night.'

Paloma pretended not to have heard and I didn't bother replying. I was looking on, lost in the chaos of that warehouse: papers piled up on the tables, open cases in empty booths (interrupted actions, like my mother's solemn toasts and the words we'd left behind). Because the border, after all, was a place to leave things behind.

A few kilometres later, with the mountains now lower, Paloma moved to the edge of her seat and stuck her head out of the window. She asked Felipe to stop, but he just accelerated harder.

'Some of us have got things to do, blondie. Hold it in.'

Paloma insisted. She was gazing up at the sky, alarmed or scared. She took my hand and pulled me in towards her so that I too could see what was going on outside. I budged over, taking up half of her seat, and lent across her. Very slowly, almost imperceptibly, the ash was vanishing before my eyes. A mirage. A big lie. The sky, which had been black, was bursting open, and very slowly I could make out white, then pale blue and then deep blue, followed by a blaze of light which would transform that day and the ones to follow. The landscape burst into colour: acacia yellow, the earthy red of the mountainsides, and green from the lush tree canopies. Felipe sat back in his seat and put his foot down, as if to flee from the reality clearly revealing itself to us: a bright, perfect sun. A terrible sun.

Paloma picked up her camera and took two or three photos: of the mountain peaks, now white again, of a poster announcing our arrival in Mendoza. She asked Felipe to slow down; it was dangerous driving like that and she couldn't get a single tree in focus. But he only accelerated harder.

'Weren't you in a hurry?' he asked her, gripping the steering wheel with all his might (red, pink, white knuckles). That glut of beautiful, peaceful views unfolding before gave me a hint of Felipe's anxiety: I didn't know how to look at that place either.

We parked the General right in front of Mendoza's main square and opted – without talking it over first, merely following the flow of cars and people – to walk around for a while first. As if we'd left another version of ourselves up in the mountains, we wandered those overly wide pavements without a care in the world: there was a hardware store, there a chemist, a sweet shop, a greengrocer, another hardware store. Felipe chased what little shade the sun afforded us (the only legible map), while Paloma, already a few metres ahead, tried to buoy us up, pointing out possible lunch spots and hotels and running her fingers through her hair to shake out the last vestiges of dust.

Having wandered aimlessly for a few blocks, we finally entered a restaurant and ordered some sandwiches and beers. As we waited I was distracted by the TV, an unwieldy old thing perched in a frame screwed to the ceiling. The international news was on, a shot of the corner of Avenida Providencia and Avenida Salvador plastered in ash.

I stood up to go to the toilet. At the end of the hallway a twisted cable, an earpiece slick with grease and a dog-eared phone directory were enticing me like buried treasure. I vacillated, hoping fate would decide whether I should make the call or just use the toilet. The sound of the flush made me opt for the phone and I asked the waitress for a few coins. She had two arms full of dirty plates, but was well-practised enough to point to two lonely coins in the tip jar. I returned to the phone without daring to look back (the TV screen, the ash, the disapproving looks), and as I listened to the dial tone I pictured the action unfolding in my mother's house: (dial tone), a jump, (dial tone), hesitation, and then the seconds she would take to get up, leave her room, contemplating the phone in dread yet wanting to pick up, like someone considering whether to throw themselves into the river or carry on across the bridge. And afterwards I pictured her answering and listening carefully, and I imagined that every word I said, each sentence that ran through that restaurant, across the streets and the *cordillera*, would remain there, forever on the other side, unpronounceable to me. Every line that slipped into my mother's house would be extinguished in there. I imagined what she was going to say (dial tone), and tried to come up with ways to explain myself (dial tone), but I couldn't think of a single excuse and, since there was no answer, I put the phone down.

I went back to the table and slipped into a trance, hypnotised by the television, enveloped in that sense of foreboding that stories of earthquakes or torrential rains always produce. Paloma and Felipe were in the middle of a heated debate, and I noticed there were two beers fewer on the table. As soon as I sat down she wanted us to cook up a plan ('*cook up*,' she said, imitating a Spanish she'd heard in cartoons).

'Let's get this over with,' she added, throwing me a complicit look I didn't know how to return. 'Let's just find her and then we can chill out here for a few days.'

Felipe took a colossal bite of his sandwich.

'So now you're in a rush, eh, Fräulein? Well I've got it all sorted out,' he said, downing the dregs of his beer.

Paloma wanted to go to the Chilean consulate.

'Right now, we're paying up and leaving right now,' she said.

She hadn't been this insistent on the way to Mendoza. Paloma had travelled calmly in the hearse as if the journey had somehow allowed her thoughts to flow freely (lost, directionless thoughts), and only now, once we were there, had her sense of urgency returned.

'It seems unlikely that anyone's going to forfeit their siesta because you've lost a coffin,' I said, surprised at how annoying I was being and longing to explain to her that, for me, merely the idea of the trip had been the trip itself, and now I had no idea what to do with all those hours ahead of us (all those hours to waste). She gave the slightest of smirks and I realised I'd lost the argument before it had even begun.

A huge house, well past its prime, with a dirty façade and a limp flag flying at half-mast (the star visible then invisible, a white hole in the middle of a fake blue sky), tallied exactly with my idea of a provincial consulate. A gate, official-looking and army green, barred access to the only entrance, and in front of the doors a guard was staving off a baying crowd, dozens strong. All lines of communication with Chile were down and they had been waiting day and night for news from their relatives from Limache, their cousins in the Andes, their nephews from Talagante and their children in Maipú.

They wanted to know what had happened to their brothers in Río Bueno, in Temuco, in San Bernardo.

'This is torture,' a woman wielding a tissue said. 'Have you no heart, young man?'

The guard pointed to a sign on his right: 'To the relatives of people affected by the situation in Chile,' (that's what it said: *the situation*) 'please return to the consulate during working hours. We appreciate your understanding, thank you.'

But nobody was moving from there. All those women and men stood waiting in front of the building. Waiting, once again (and for a second I thought the ash would start to fall on it): a throng of people sharing sandwiches, camomile teas, sharing their never-ending sorrows. There were fathers looking thin and waving their fists, some steeped in a thick air of resignation, others at the end of their tether. And the mothers, the majority mothers, those stoical mothers who defied the guard with their deep cries, almost howls; thin-lipped mothers, women with their nails bitten right down, keeping one another company, linked at the arm, desperate, willing to sacrifice it all (and in my head I heard the telephone blaring: 'I do all this for you, Iquela').

I convinced Paloma there was no point in staying: the consulate wasn't open and our only option was to go back the following day ('the normal channels, Paloma, the forms'). I spoke with conviction, but really all I could think about was the sign, the phone lines that were down, my mother drenching the garden with her hose. I imagined her dialling my mobile number over and over again only to hear an out-of-service message, and I wanted to call her again and tell her, once and for all, 'Consuelo, it's me, I'm not going to bring her to you. I don't know where Ingrid is, please forgive me. I don't know where to look for all those things of yours,

Mum, all those things from back then.' And then I thought about telling Paloma to stay on in Mendoza with me a few days, to spend nights, weeks, our whole lives there, to forget about everything. Absolutely everything. At the same time, though, I longed for the opposite: to go home (to return to Chile, to repatriate myself).

We spent the rest of the evening tramping the same streets. Paloma seemed resigned to wait and Felipe walked up ahead with her to avoid having to be alone with me, as if our argument from the night before was lingering there and might spark up again with just one small slip. I was deep in my own thoughts. It was no longer the ash that seemed make-believe now but the absence of it: the clean streets, the blue sky and the blasted sun like a scab rooted right in its centre.

Just before night fell, close to the Plaza del Castillo, we decided to try our luck with a hotel. Clearly an elegant building not so long ago, the only remnants of its former glory were the two marble plant pots by the entrance and a faded carpeted staircase. It was called Mendoza In (like that, one n) and on first sight it seemed half-empty. The reception consisted of a large salon and a woman sitting behind the desk, inspecting her nails. Her hair was cut short, shaved on one side, and her nails were bitten down and painted black. Behind her stood a cabinet with about twenty pigeonholes, each one with a room key hanging from a hook. Felipe and I stood in front of her and waited.

'We've got triples, doubles, twins and singles,' the woman said without looking up from her nails. Her voice sounded familiar to me.

'Can I help you then?' she asked, and that slow, deep drawl carried me far away, to the deep voice of another who

smoked a lot and shouted too much. It took me back to when
I had braces and a flat chest, to the day I came home to find
the white van parked up in front of the house, went in with
my jumper dirty with wet patches under my arms and found
Felipe's grandma sitting in an armchair next to my mother,
saying, while looking at me up and down, her wrinkly old
hands cupping a mug of tea: 'Is that Iquela all grown up?'
(her voice and then the longest silence, a parenthesis that
held no words). Yes, I told her, of course it was me. She went
on inspecting me and told my mother that I still looked like
a boy. And I stood there blushing but with a smile painted
across my face, waiting for instructions, for a sign, for my
mother to protect me with some words of solidarity. But
without looking at me my mother just nodded. Consuelo
clenched fists and through gritted teeth just replied that I
was still a child.

'They're such naïve children, Elsa.'

'Two months or so,' his Grandma Elsa had said, but now,
in Mendoza, it was Felipe who spoke.

'Two nights, thank you very much,' and he booked two
rooms and clipped me around the head. 'Snap out of it,
Iquela.' I must have had my pensive face on, or my counting
face, or my thinking-about-bullshit face, all of them amount-
ing to the same thing.

Paloma wanted to know what had happened between
us. She came over pulling her case, all ready to go up to the
room, and then stood, waiting for the reason behind Felipe's
mocking smirk. He was quick to answer on my behalf.

'Nothing's wrong with her,' he said, 'she's just stuck in
the past.'

I could feel my face flushing, the skin responding to Felipe
that *he* was the obsessive one, that running away was pathetic.

But my words were caught somewhere between my chest and my throat, a rough ball of words, an intractable barrier, as if the woman with the black nails had lodged them there with her eyes, the same eyes that were now staring at us, either out of bemusement or curiosity, from the other side of the desk, watching as Felipe put on a squeaky high voice to say, 'she'll be thinking about her mum, her mummy, her mummywummy, her mummikins'.

I didn't mean to say the raw words that came streaming out then, the ones I should have left on the other side of the border. They simply burst out of me, flooding everything. I just didn't care any more; or at least, I thought I didn't.

'Look who's talking,' I said to Felipe, moulding each syllable out of my rage. 'Mr Light and Breezy, *so* at peace with the past.'

And Felipe, with his black eyes, with a squinting gaze just like his grandma's, my mother's, and perhaps like that of his own parents, snapped back:

'And what exactly does the prodigal daughter mean by that?'

Lines poured out of me like an oil spill, like grease, like lava that *did* burn, that *did* hurt.

'I mean that you don't even have to open your mouth: it's written all over your face.' That's what I said to him. 'It's written all over your face, Felipe.'

And just like that the rest of my words withdrew, repentant (black nails galloping against the marble: dead petals falling from the fingers). Paloma edged in nervously, the previous night's disbelief now gone. She tried to come between us, to separate us with cold, liquid words, safe words that only cut deeper.

'What's written all over his face?'

I looked down at the floor. We never spoke about that. It was a childhood pact, from way back, when he and I had been sitting on the woollen rug pretending to play, pretending that we couldn't hear, that nothing was going on in the living room while my mother and his gran yelled at one another and we couldn't help but listen in, couldn't help but find out my mother *had* to look after him, as a debt:

'It's the least you can do for me,' his Grandma Elsa had said. 'This is your fault, Consuelo, all your fault. If you lot hadn't gone off playing war this never would have happened to my Felipe. It must have been something you did. That's right, all of you lot who are still alive, you did something.' And my mother tried to explain that it wasn't her fault.

'You don't understand, Elsa. It was terrible. It was a mistake.'

And the mistake was not even hers. The mistake had been my father's (Rodolfo's, Victor's: Victor had made a mistake), for muttering two little words when they captured him, two words that, like a mistranslation, a slip of the tongue, changed everything. He'd said 'Felipe Arrabal': name and surname, two words to erase a body. But Felipe didn't know that and supposedly nor did I, and maybe it didn't even matter, or at least that's what we wanted to believe and we made a promise not to talk about it; we swore that we would forget all about it, unremember anything to do with that past we hadn't even lived through but remembered in too perfect detail for it to be made up.

And there we were, Felipe and I, in that hotel lobby, and my words had betrayed me and I couldn't take them back (names, surnames, razor-sharp vowels that spill out and get stuck to your feet).

'What's written all over his face?' I heard again.

Felipe walked right up to Paloma, leaving no more than a centimetre between his nose and hers.

'That we're all dead, Fräulein. Dead-dead,' he said, and he took one of the keys on the reception desk and bounded up the stairs, two, even three at a time, laughing loudly, the laugh he used to stop himself from crying. Or maybe not: maybe he really was laughing and I was the one who wanted to cry.

(I do all this for you I do all this for you I do all this for you
I do all this for you I do all this for you I do all this for you
I do all this for you I do all this for you I do all this for you
I do all this for you I do all this for you I do all this for you
I do all this for you I do all this for you I do all this for you
I do all this for you.)

Written all over my face or not, since when was she so
opinionated? now those two are fooling around they've got
all big for their boots, dishing out opinions like they're paid
per word, when really the only thing they're doing is getting
in the way of my calculations because this isn't a honeymoon,
no sir, I'm working here, working out if there are any more
dead to subtract, but with all this fresh air I get muddled,
my mind clouds over, which is why I bring all my eyes into
focus, to cut through the mental fog and see if there are any
more mislaid stiffs lying around, cos they could be anywhere:
in the pollen of the hydrangeas, in the spikes on the cacti,
in the salt crystals in the desert, and that's why I head out
into Mendoza, to see if I can air all these black thoughts:
written all over my face or not, what difference does it make
when the one who's really hung up is her, Iquela, while I,
on the other hand, just keep on moving, walking and looking round me, cos time is a traitor, like Iquela, hell-bent on
making sure they can't tell, that it's not written all over her
face, when really the rage pours out of her eyes, yeah, that's
why I told her when we were kids to walk with her eyes to
the ground, to avoid the gaze of her living-dead dad, to listen
less to her mummy, to talk always to stray dogs and meadowlarks, cos I learnt to read the lies in corneas, not mouths,

and, well, mouths are silky and smooth and I don't like smooth things, no, that's why I trained myself to make out the rage in the pupils of dogs and cows, those southern cows with their grey eyes, because they weren't white and smooth those eyes, no, they were a pair of slippery, greyish sclera, the whites of the eye, only, in this case, they were grey, identical to the eye they brought me in Biology once, an eye that smelt bad but whose look gave away everything, it was written all over that eye: the choroids, the fovea and the blind spot, yeah, that wondrous eye our teacher brought one morning, one each, she told me and Iquela, the Iquela from our childhood, not so cool then, no, a total loner, just one friend, that other girl, the weirdo who'd follow her round school like a shadow, that little mouse of a thing who was always digging her nail into Iquela's hand, her friend the scratcher, while now Iquela walks around with her chest puffed up thinking she's the bee's knees; it wasn't like that before, which is why I'd sit with her, cos I'd promised and promises are debts and you always pay your debts, I sat right next to her in that classroom, each of us waiting for our own eye, but at the last minute the teacher told us he was sorry, very sorry, but there weren't enough eyes, there are never enough eyes, and so I had to share, an eye per pair the teacher told us, and I was really mad but I swallowed my rage because there it was, there it was in the middle of that enormous classroom, lying on the lino table, so whole and big and beautiful, there was the eye, it was staring at me, and I edged nervously towards it, but straight away I knew that it was mine, that eye was fixed on me, because it looked like a hamster, a street rat, a burnt-out star on the table, and Iquela and I were sitting right next to each other, Iquela, the eye and me, and then I cupped it in my hands and held it like

141

a rabbit, I held it up and brought it in close to inspect it, without blinking, eye to eye, and in its dilated pupil I saw half of everything that cow had ever seen: I saw black patches on white coats, I saw the blazing red iron bearing down, I saw placenta and blood and a squidgy mass coming out of its entrails, I saw thick, yellowy milk and rusty machines sucking on its udders, and I saw the creamy top, that creamy skin, and white aprons splattered with red, and I also saw lovely things like the mud encrusted in its hooves and the dew dusting its ears, and the clouds rolling over his back, stroking it, and stroking mine too, stroking me, all this I saw split in two while my hands took the vitreous humour and squeezed it, disgusted, cos I find smooth things disgusting, yeah, but I went on looking anyway, because the cow had imagined lovely things: it had dreamt of tall, wild meadows and flies rubbing their legs together against their neck, and it had seen sad things, things that had saddened it like the parched fields and dried-up well, and at the end of all this I saw a long line of other cows, tail to mouth, that's how they were, perfectly in line, and at the end of the passage I saw a light, the gleaming flash of blades, knives lit under halogen, slicing against one another, a terrible shrill ringing, yeah, and you couldn't see it in the round eyes of any of those cows, their sorrow and their fear weren't written all over their faces, which is why I went on looking, and then the parts appeared: the hunks hanging upside down, legs, necks, flayed feet, the horrible hunks of this cow, ribs, hooves, and I kept looking in spite of it all, in spite of the disgust and the fear I kept observing that eye, cos the cow and I had seen similar things, that's what I thought as I touched the white-grey sclera and its reddish constellations, its skeletal veins and iris scored with scars, and then I raised my eyes and saw Iquela sort of hypnotised, clutching the scalpel and carefully extracting the lens, telling me to touch the optic nerve, see what it feels like, she was saying, and then, first making sure no one could see her, she removed her gloves to touch the soft part and sniff her fingers, Iquela did that, I saw her, she sniffed her fingers and then sucked them one after the other while I looked around and removed the cornea and I took it, I did that and nobody saw me, and the teacher gave us a four out of ten for being messy, and that night, when Consuelo and the living-dead man had gone to sleep, I slipped into Iquela's room and showed her the cornea, look what I've brought you, Ique, it's ours, for both of us, so we always see the same things, even if we're far away, half for you and half for me, I said holding it out like treasure in my hand, but she said, no way, José, that's gross, because Iquela only has one set of brown eyes, eyes made for seeing her mum, her mummy, her mummakins, and she says that it's written all over *my* face, ha! I'm the only one who does anything useful around here, indispensable things like finding dead people and subtracting them, how can my sorrow be written all over my face with all these eyes, because everyone knows that you grieve through the eyes and I've got hundreds, millions of them, cos even though Iquela didn't want her share of the cornea, I didn't care and I trundled off to the bathroom alone, locked the door, took out the cornea and placed that soft mulch on the tip of my tongue, that's what I did, because I wanted to see what was inside me, because I couldn't feel anything, no, and you keep your feelings on the inside, which is why I stuck out my tongue with the cornea and I looked at myself for a while in the mirror, and from the tip of my tongue I saw half my face and half of everything I'd ever seen: stray, hungry pups and every one of my decapitated flowers, the petals, the sepals and the stamens strewn on the ground, the chickens coming back to life, and hundreds of bones at the bottoms of black pits; I saw long-tailed meadowlarks, giant crunchy *nalcas*, and all my unfinished subtractions, and my Gran Elsa and Don Francisco and my mother dying again, and also my dad, but not whole, no, there were his parts, parts, parts, and I've never liked the parts, which is why in the end I swallowed it, just like that, without so much as a swig of water, and the cornea was salty and as it slipped down my throat I saw all those new landscapes inside me; I saw the soft walls I was made up of as the thing made its way sadly along the thick wet bends of my body, travelling through my pink waters, and I saw poo and blood clots and tattered muscles, and I also saw lost ideas, night-time ideas cowering from the day; and then came the black and everything dissolved, because the cornea was pulverised and turned into millions of particles floating in my blood, and each of those particles snuck into my pores and that's how the eyes in my skin came about, and that's why I see them, cos I have a completely different perspective, in each pore a minuscule eye born of that cornea, and given how many there are I can spot dead bodies wherever they are, and here in this town there are none, no, the only thing here in Mendoza is air, so much air that I'm choking, so much air that all I want to do is smoke, smoke a spliff and for its fumes to make me disappear, to take a drag and vanish whole, to breathe in and not feel the oxygen, because there's way too much oxygen here, yeah, way too much air.

( )

It happened not long after we buried my father, back when I would spend entire afternoons glued to my bedroom window telling people, perfectly calmly, that I felt fine, absolutely fine. Felipe and I went to the same school that winter and at the end of one break time, a few minutes before the bell called us back to class, he froze on the spot in silence, his eyes fixed on some kids playing a few metres away from us. It was his idea and he wouldn't shut up about it.

'Let's collect scabs, Ique. We need to give the other pain a break. Choose one of them, Ique, any one,' he said, pointing to a group of girls skipping together. 'Choose one and sock it to her,' he went on, aiming his hand like a gun at a fat, red-headed kid who was in goal and sweating profusely. 'Smash her nose in, Ique. Pull her eyes out of her sockets. Stick pins under her nails. Clench your fist, close your mind and just punch. And don't worry,' he whispered in my ear, hammering home each syllable, 'self-defence is a reflex and they're definitely going to hit you harder.'

I told him I wasn't interested in fighting. I didn't know how to punch, and besides, I felt fine (nothing, I felt nothing). But there was no dissuading him. Felipe looked straight through me as if seeing me for the first and last time, like a stranger, and he didn't utter another word. Gathering himself and shutting those eyes (shutting his mouth, shutting himself off entirely) he shoved me with all his weight, and the next thing I felt was the ground under my body. My head hit the concrete and my hands scraped the gritty asphalt. I heard the dull thump of my back against the ground. I opened my eyes. The excited faces of dozens of children were arranged in a circle around me: the redhead was crying with laughter; three older kids were pointing at me. I saw lots of tiny teeth, some stained, and heard shouts that sounded like they were coming from a fight near me, no, over me, across my body, because Felipe had thrown himself on top of me and, still staring through me with those blank eyes of his, he hit me like nobody has ever hit me before. He pulled my hair with all his might. He kneed me in the stomach. He drove his fist right into my chest. Only after a few seconds did my instincts start to kick in. I struggled desperately to free myself, to make him unclench his fists and release his knee lock, and when at last I was able to wriggle out from beneath him, I took a deep breath (dirt, snot, fear), I took a deep, deep breath, turned around and using every ounce of strength I had (a dangerous strength I hadn't known I had), I hauled myself on top of him, pinned him down and with my eyes open, not thinking about what I was doing but moving exactly as he'd told me, swiftly and sharply, I hit him as you could only hit someone you really love. Now I was pulling his hair and scratching his arms. I sunk my nails into his face, buried my knees into his groin and my teeth into his shoulder. I hit him until I felt nothing but a sharp pain and a sticky dampness on the palms of my hands and all over my hot, mucky face. He didn't move once. It wasn't true what he'd told me: self-defence isn't a reflex. Felipe remained still with his eyes open, enjoying it, as if by receiving my punches and spits he felt less alone. Cradled in my rage, covered in dirt and blood and breathing very slowly, Felipe just smiled. Nobody separated us. It was purely the exhaustion, after so much, that forced me to stop and slump down at his side. My knuckles were burning and I felt an uncontainable burst of sadness. We never spoke of our fight, but something was sealed in that moment, in the long pause in which he and I caught our breath as the other kids moved away, disappointed, and the branches of some reddish trees swayed in the breeze above us.

And there, cooped up in the hearse, in that hearse that had become our roving home, on that simulacrum of a search that had brought us together again, one last time, lying in wait for that dead woman, accelerating to escape the terrible blue sky and listening to the distant rustle of leaves, I was struck down by a very similar feeling of vertigo.

As we approached the cargo area at the airport, after a morning spent in silence, feigning a truce, I spotted a man guarding the entry to the runway. He was wearing orange high-vis overalls, a black beanie hat and enormous headphones to protect him from the noise of the turbines. He was waiting in a cabin next to a metal barrier, which he raised to let through a tanker and then closed again the moment he saw us heading that way. A sign warned us that it wouldn't be an easy job persuading him: RESTRICTED AREA. AUTHORISED PERSONNEL ONLY. Felipe stopped the car and Paloma asked me to speak to the man; she was too wound up, and, after all, it had been my idea to come to the airport.

The man looked me up and down, a look that forced me to search for some kind of sign (a raw word stuck to my mouth), and he didn't bother greeting me. Acting as naturally as I could, albeit with a forced grin, I asked him where we could find the cargo from the cancelled flights (it seemed better to say 'cargo' than 'remains', 'cadaver', 'dead woman', 'Ingrid'). He didn't say anything for a long time and I kept talking to fill the awkward silence, telling him that this situation with the ash demanded an urgent response and that the daughter had travelled from Germany, no less. He rubbed his chin and frowned.

'What situation?' he shouted over the roar of nearby engines.

'The ash in Chile,' I replied, raising my voice (an inaudible voice).

'Say again?' And from the pocket of his overalls he removed a packet of cigarettes, lit one and let himself be engulfed in a large cloud of smoke, which was nothing for those of us who'd come from the other side of the *cordillera*. I insisted we'd travelled all that way precisely for this reason, to pick up the remains of a woman.

'Ingrid . . .' I said, surprised at my block, my blank, which Paloma took no time to fill.

'Ingrid Aguirre,' she said leaning out of the hearse window. Aguirre.

Until that moment she hadn't had a surname. All those stories were either about Rodolfo, Consuelo, Ingrid, Hans or all those other names: Víctor, Claudia, those doubles of our parents from back before they were parents. Rootless names with no antecedents or surnames, which made them feel fictional, lent them a certain lightness that allowed me to believe, if only for a second, that the whole thing had been one big lie. Only characters from novels had *just* a first name. A Víctor or a Claudia alone couldn't exist. Ingrid Aguirre, on the other hand, really had died.

The security guard's face was scaring me. I was afraid he would tell us where she was, or that he would point to a coffin in the middle of the runway (an errant coffin doing the rounds in the empty hangars). I was afraid of finding her and having to go back to Chile, where I'd tell my mother that I had her friend, her comrade, her Ingrid Aguirre. The man raised his right arm (and I thought his finger was pointing somewhere, to the end of our search).

'Papers,' he said, holding out his palm to Paloma, who was leaning half her body over Felipe. 'Did you bring the form?'

And then I remembered the established procedure, the normal channels, the rules about repatriating the mortal remains of a deceased person. We didn't have any papers, and no papers meant no body.

'I can't give you any information,' the man said before closing his open hand and the barrier that would have given us access.

'Oh, that's all I needed,' Felipe snapped, before hitting the steering wheel.

'*Scheiße*,' Paloma said.

I did my best to hide my relief and suggested we return to the city as soon as possible. It made no sense to harass the guard, who by now was shooing us away with his hand, telling us to clear the entrance.

We drove back to the centre of town and wandered around Mendoza, unsure what to do next. People were out walking their dogs, walking their children, walking their dogs *and* their children (with no ash or dead mothers or mothers who wouldn't answer the phone). Everything appeared suspiciously normal, though Felipe still wasn't talking to me and Paloma had that doleful look again. She seemed dejected, wrapped in the grief that kept swinging her back and forth between disbelief and despair. Perhaps by this point she was regretting having travelled to Chile instead of burying Ingrid in Berlin, in a cemetery where her surname was unique, where it would be easy to spot her tombstone among the others. Or perhaps she was regretting not having cremated her and brought her ashes back to Chile on the plane. Who knows. Ash on top of ashes would have been too much.

I seemed to be the only one capable of enjoying that stroll. We would spend at least one more day in Mendoza (one more day with no phones, no pouring ash, no eight and a half blocks to cover), so I moved cheerfully from one street to the next, marvelling aloud at the width of the pavements, so wide for such a small city, and commenting on the buses, the turtle doves, the poplars, the shops. But there was no distracting Paloma. Even when I went in to give her a hug I got nothing more than a discouraging stiff smile in return.

We were entering San Martín Park, through two huge monumental doors, when I decided to give it one last shot. Moving right next to Paloma, I told her in a concerned voice that maybe her mother had been mislaid, that maybe, just maybe, she wouldn't be able to bury her in Santiago after all and that we should wait for the bad weather to pass before carrying on the search. Paloma picked up her step, leaving me trailing metres behind (and I counted three sparrows taking flight from a gnarled old cypress). Only as evening began to fall, after more than an hour spent wandering around the park, did Felipe break his ridiculous vow of silence from the night before to suggest that we find a bar.

'No time to waste, I say,' he said, 'And besides, the air here is weird. Can't you feel it?' and he flapped away some non-existent insects with his hand.

'There's too much of it,' I replied, and he nodded.

'Too much air, that's it,' and he walked off in the direction of a woman who was smoking near the park's exit. Her lips were painted dark red and appeared almost black in the darkness, making her look sullen, and her mouth seemed to come unstuck from her face with every puff on her cigarette (and her lips remained imprinted on the filter: woman with mouth, woman without mouth). Felipe asked her for a cigarette, but not even his winning smile could do the trick. She refused and pointed towards a door where, she said, 'we could buy anything we could possibly want'.

The wooden door led us to a second door, this time made of tin, which was dented at foot level, clearly having received its fair share of kicks. On the other side, tucked away, was a dingy underground bar that reeked of sweet and sour, beer-soaked floor, and where it felt like three in the morning.

The barman bombarded us with questions as he made our drinks. He took a bottle off the half-empty shelf behind him and, without even looking at the glass, he poured out perfect measures of whisky by heart and asked us if we were Chilean, what we were doing, where our boyfriends and girlfriends were, such a good-looking bunch, what a waste.

Paloma was quick to point out that she was German and didn't add much else. Instead, she wandered off in the direction of a pool table and gestured at me to follow her. We drank our first whisky there while deciding whether to play a game or simply watch Felipe, who had now draped half his body over the bar and was in deep conversation with the barman. They had to shout to hear one another, and they laughed as the man passed Felipe an array of bottles, which he sniffed suspiciously. At one point they shook hands and the man handed him a packet of cigarettes and a bottle of *aguardiente*. Felipe served himself a glass, refilled it twice more and then made a beeline for Paloma, offering her the bottle directly to her mouth.

'This tune's dedicated to you,' he said, removing the camera, which I hadn't even noticed, from around her neck.

I recognised the drums, and I noticed a woman was watching us from afar. I remembered her black nails, which she now was tapping on the bar, and I waved at her and smiled. She was looking through me, at something behind me: a very pale and thoughtful Felipe was over-egging his drunken state and crooning, or rather wailing, along to the song and playing with the zoom on Paloma's camera. He came over to me and bellowed in my ear as if all the voices in his head had woken up and he was trying, unsuccessfully, to impose his own. I don't remember what he said, just his hands holding my face, drawing it in towards his, pulling me towards him and the blaring music drowning out his words despite his mouth moving right in front me. I guessed he was talking about our argument, but that didn't matter any more.

'Forget it, Felipe,' I shouted, recoiling from his cold hands and taking two swigs of *aguardiente*. 'It doesn't matter,' I said, and I watched as the woman with the black nails approached us and draped her body all over Felipe, rubbing up against him and then taking Paloma's hand to whisper a word in her ear. Paloma was dancing with her eyes closed in the middle of the bar, her arms raised high and her hips swaying. I went up to her with more enthusiasm than I felt, trying to get into it by following her lead, but it was useless. She was dancing out of time, following a secret, internal rhythm completely at odds with the music. The woman went back to the bar and I felt Paloma's hand grab my wrist and watched her take Felipe's arm, pulling us both towards her. We left the main room and headed down a corridor. Paloma locked the door behind us and switched on the bright lights (interrogation lights).

The song faded into the background and we found ourselves huddled together in a cramped toilet, the smell thick and bodily, paper spilling over the bin, wallpaper plastered in graffiti, shit marks in a toilet with no seat and a maddening dripping sound. Paloma said she had a surprise for us ('just a little one,' she said, making light of it) and with a wicked glint in her eyes she opened her rucksack slowly and pulled out a round wad: a navy ball of thick socks. Felipe and I exchanged glances. Paloma was lapping up the attention, a wide smile spreading across her face to reveal some tiny teeth, as well as the silver barbell in the middle of her tongue.

She took that blue ball and unpeeled it very carefully, ceremoniously, standing before us as if we were about to behold the miracle of the five thousand. Finally, deep down in the centre of the ball, a silvery object appeared: a tiny, doll-sized bottle.

'Well, what do we have here?' Felipe asked, snatching the bottle from her hands and swilling it around so that its contents formed a vortex like an enormous tornado.

'One of my mum's potions, for her cancer,' Paloma replied, but I heard something else. I didn't hear 'potions', I heard 'poisons', 'one of my mum's poisons', and the bottle remained firmly in Felipe's hand, the liquid a mad whirlpool.

Felipe asked Paloma what kind of potion it was, what kind of drug, what did it do. He was trying to decipher the German on the label, with its red circle crossed out, its health warning. Paloma didn't answer. She looked at me smugly, squinting her eyes as she had done all those years earlier, and then took the bottle back off Felipe, held it up, toasted the air and without even pulling a face, she drank more than a third of the liquid.

'Prost,' she said.

One of her mum's potions. A poison she'd brought with her in an attempt to get rid of everything, to make sure she was left with no trace of her mother. Or maybe she'd stolen it before Ingrid died, to drink a toast, to cure herself. Felipe snatched the little bottle back out of her hands, closed his eyes, took two sips and passed it to me. The liquid inside the bottle was still whirling around. I held it to my nose (an innocuous smell), and without a second thought I downed what was left. The dregs, the remains, that's what I took: the sweet remains with a bitter aftertaste, so bitter it stripped the inside of my mouth and made me clench my eyes together.

Nothing for the first few seconds. Everything existed in perfect balance. I asked Paloma what kind of cancer her mum had died of.

'You're about to find out,' she replied, but now another person entirely was speaking, a voice wrapped in cotton wool. 'Hold on a minute and you'll see what kind of cancer it was.'

A second went by, and another, and another. I read the scribbles on the wall. *Pequi, I luv you. What r u lookin at? Get the fuck outta here.* I wanted to know the exact illness in order to guess at the remedy: what did you take to cure confused, upset cells? I wanted to know what Paloma wanted to cure us from. *Get the fuck outta here.* What did you take to offset those invasive cells? *What r u looking at?* Then, all of a sudden, something happened to the walls, to the smell, to the brightness of the light.

The tips of my fingers. The same sensation as those mornings when certain parts of my body don't want to wake up and stay numb. My fingertips, hands, wrists, all numb. A faint dizziness. My arms, then my neck and chest. My entire body was withdrawing, coming away from me, or perhaps I was the one abandoning my body in order to float a few centimetres above it.

'Nice, eh?'

A warm current heating me up, erasing me.

'Oh you've really outdone yourself, blondie.'

My blood slower and thicker, the colours brighter. The colours.

'Take a look at those colours, Fräulein. She must have had cancer of the everything.'

(Cancer of the eyelids, the eardrums, the nails.)

I told Paloma I wasn't feeling anything, but when I spoke I heard another voice coming out of me. She remained silent, her freckles blue, her yellow eyes saying incomprehensible things, letters hanging on the walls, hanging from the threads of a language I wasn't taking in, or rather couldn't, because I didn't understand it. Nor could I read all the messages being shouted by the walls. Everything was a blur; those walls were spying on me and I myself was as light as vapour. I couldn't count the objects around me. My thoughts were slipping away from me. Not feeling a thing: the remedy for that illness.

Felipe went to turn out the light but Paloma stopped him. I thought I heard her say, 'Let's watch the fire', but I couldn't be sure. She came over to me, took my hand, held it up to her face and slipped two of my fingers in her mouth. I should have felt her soft tongue, the slippery steel of the barbell buried there, but what I felt was the opposite: her fingers inside *my* mouth, that screw driving into *my* tongue. She moved in slow motion, touching my arms and hands that seemed no longer to belong to me, all the while staring at me with a neutral expression, freckles dotted all over her forehead. Felipe was muttering unintelligible commentaries, something about how good the water was, the dry water, he said before falling quiet again, also coming over to me, where he took me by the back of my neck and kissed me. I thought I felt the graze of his moustache, the tension of his lips against mine, or maybe it was something else. Maybe he kissed Paloma and that kiss landed on my lips, or it was the swirling lights that kissed me, kissed and obliterated me (swirls of lights that lit me up, that set me alight).

'Look at me,' Felipe said then and I looked up and saw his arms and hands shaking, about to shatter into a million splinters. 'Look at me,' he repeated, out of himself and shaking. He wasn't speaking to me or Paloma. 'Look at me,' he screamed, and I realised he was talking to the mirror. 'Look at me, for fuck's sake. Written all over my face, is it?'

Paloma went over to him as if the order had been directed at her. She appeared in the reflection, but without her eyes; she aimed and pushed the button on the camera, the only solid object now in that toilet, making the same sound over and over. Click. Click. Click. (Three wasted seconds.) Click. Click. Click. And Felipe went on spitting the same order at his own reflection.

'Look at me.'

I floated towards that mirror until his face appeared. His two eyes weren't quite in line, his eyebrows were arched and black, and his dark skin was flaky around the nose, that aquiline nose that was ever so slightly too big for his face. His pupils were dilated, couched within his glassy, slanting eyes, and his skin was incredibly firm and soft, with no beard or moustache. That's what I saw. Not a trace of that new moustache on his face. Because it wasn't Felipe's adult face that I saw looking back at him from the mirror; it was his pinker, rounder face, his childhood face. That's what I saw and I was scared. I couldn't feel it in my stomach, but I could sense my fear. Nonetheless, I put it to one side and carried on moving in, desperate to see myself, convinced that I would find myself locked inside that mirror: my taut black mane, my drowsy eyes, my sad eyes observing me from the other side of the mirror. And, despite my fear, I moved in closer still. I moved in until I was standing directly in front of the mirror. I stopped right next to Felipe and with my heart pounding in my chest, with my mouth dry and hands clenched, I opened my eyes (I longed to count myself, take stock of myself, to reinvent myself).

But I wasn't there.

There was nobody looking back at me.

2

Dipping my tongue into a delicious juice and feeling it turn to scalding water, sandpaper water, lava water, bad water blazing in my mouth, and it chafes like a stubbly beard, like a thousand thorns, a rough mouth which my tongue glides across, my tongue bleeding as I burn up, set myself on fire with the liquid that looks cold but it burns; you can't tell, but it burns as it runs down my throat, my windpipe, as harsh as the lights in here, as the splintered rays pricking my eyes, poking my eyes with their long needles, following me out of the bathroom: piss off, leave me alone, and I look at Iquela but she doesn't see me, she doesn't see me cos her eyes have dropped to the sky and from there I can't pin them to their sockets, eyes popped out of their sockets with no pins to hold them in place and so they float and I float, I levitate with the white liquid and rise up towards the light, yeah, the square of light shining above the bar, the light showing ash over Santiago, would you look at Plaza Italia, what a mess, and the lens is dirty and the zoom goes in and out and in again and turns black, because someone switches off the TV, and I switch off too and then the music starts, a shrill song, harsh on the ears, harsh as angles, shrill as those howling dogs, shrill and harsh like the wailing of the ambulance and all those midday thoughts, and the big day is

approaching because that dead man was thirty-one, yeah,
but there are no dead here and I'm thirsty, that's the only
thing I do have, a reddish thirst, which is why I want more
of that bitter liquid, that healing elixir, give me more, Paloma,
where are you? don't be a drag, but the German isn't here,
the German who wanted to cure us has gone again and left
me without a drop of antidote, just the little bottle, round
and empty, which held the remedy that swirled in a whirlpool, the kind of whirlpool I like because they don't stop, I
hate things that stop, I like the never-ending stories, the
enduring stories, yeah, like the rubber trees and weeping
figs and the whirlpools of the Mapocho, though in fact the
Mapocho doesn't have any whirlpools, because you can't
even make out the banks or the start of the water, and cos
no one wants to take that river seriously, no one except me,
I want to stir it up till I've made a tornado to twizzle and
twirl above a giant cup, all the water in the Mapocho falling
in a waterfall I swirl around and around and then drink,
boom, I drink the liquid with the corollas and the puppy-
eyed mongrels, their dark watery eyes looking up at me and
their paws scratching my face, eh, *Chileno*, you alright there?
and I can't feel my skin or my osso buco bones, just splinters
and my chapped lips, hey, give that kid a glass of water, he's
as pale as a ghost, and my throat disappears, and then my
windpipe then my stomach and I can't feel my balls or my
thighs, and then my black thoughts and my calculations
vanish too, tell that *Chileno* kid to come over to the bar, here,
come on, come on, take a seat, cos I'm drowning in the whirl
of dirty water and I'm cured, yeah, and my thoughts turn
soft like pink bubblegum, my thoughts stretch and mould
to my skull, which is tingling, there's ants all over the place,
bloody hell, everything's crawling, the whole planet's

shaking because I can't feel a thing, not the whole or the parts, I can't feel what's real or what's fake, I can't feel anything and I'm off my head, yeah, cos the German's potion has taken me to a higher plane and my eyelids are curtains, and inside my black ideas light up, but I want to hide them cos there's a man at the bar, yeah, a man with ants crawling over his arms and on his top lip, and those black black ants are freaking me out, you OK, *Chileno*?, and the ants dance and the voices are splinters and the words are buried deep inside my pupils where they clash with my black thoughts sending sparks flying, and I cover my eyes with my hands to hide them and to hide myself and then they explode, yeah, my eyes explode into hundreds and thousands of skies, take a deep breath, that's it, breathe, *Chileno*, but I don't want to breathe, I want to scream, howl as loudly as I can, but my voice has gone, I can't find it, it's hiding in the shadow of my tonsils, and it's blended in with those stupid black night thoughts, fuck, what's up, I can't see, I'm off my head, and the water in the glass they bring me is thick and dry and the man touches me, he touches my shoulder and it reappears, deep breath, that's it, my shoulder is back, it exists, and so do the other parts of my body, and the air is a saw cleaving me, opening me up, thaaat's it, keep drinking water, *Chileno*, and the guy looks at me and I draw back the curtains of the hundreds of eyes all over me and I know him, I know I've seen this man, yeah, and I take a deep breath and the water is sweet now, sweet and dry and the man is smiling, better, *Chileno*? you've lost that dead-man-walking look you had going there for a while, and his teeth are glow-worms that have gone out, and everything in me goes out, looks like they've left you on your lonesome, and it's true, they've left me lonelier than a ghost, cos Iquela isn't here and the German's on another planet, she's lucky to have made it to Santiago at all, how'd you get along with that cargo you were after? and the Argentinian is asking me about some kind of cargo and I don't know what he means, you know, don't play dumb, and I shrug my shoulders, cos I've got shoulders again, and I furrow my brow, cos I have a brow, and behind it there are thoughts and those thoughts are orange, orange thoughts, orange, orange, orange overalls man from the airport, yeah! I see him and I know it's him, it's the guard in front of me, the guard from the barrier, yeah, and the black ants go crazy cos I recognise them, I see them under that hooked nose, I've identified them and they no longer scare me, and he asks if I found what I was look-ing for in the airport and now I know he's referring to the stiff, to the fugitive, to that stubborn corpse, another round? and this new liquid is made of gold and the dead lady isn't here, the deceased isn't here and I have to subtract her, I listen, and I know I'm the one talking, it's my voice speak-ing, it's had enough of playing hide-and-seek, it's rebelling against the potion, the cure, it comes back to say subtract her, subtract her, I repeat, and the man is talking fast but I don't hear him, cos it's his eyelashes and his nostrils speak-ing to me, he's speaking from his orange overalls, from his skin and red bones, he's speaking to me because the ants are scrambling all over his lips, they're saying sure, *Chileno*, go and look, people should be buried where they belong, he says, and the glass of gold liquid is suddenly full of black ants, and we sure have our fair share of dead here, he says, too-too-ma-ny, but I can't be sure if he says this or nothing at all, if he's telling me to look for her tomorrow, early in the morning, hangar number seven, *Chileno*, will you remem-ber? and I repeat seven, seven, seven, hangar number seven, yeah, but I say it in my head because it's gone again, my voice has gone walkabout, crouching in among the hundreds of eyes on my skin and the millions of black ideas, my voice hiding inside my bones and I feel a terrible chill run through me, like a rock-hard river rushing up me from the soles of my feet, a surge of cement rising up from my heels, a tidal wave that numbs my calves and knees and thighs and balls, and the cement climbs up to my stomach and freezes my chest and turns my neck stiff and makes me clench my teeth to stop myself from vomiting, you feeling alright, *Chileno*?, and I just vomit, yeah, vomit till there's nothing left, till there's no thirty-year-old dead man left, no body, no corpse, no stiff, yeah, till there's no whisky or wine or water, till there are no potions or white liquids, no saliva, no bile or blood, till there are no more corpses or ash, or bars with razor-sharp saws floating around; throw up and purge myself of days as red as my vomit, red like lava should be, the lava that isn't here, that's never been here, because we don't know where it comes from, this bitter, hot liquid, this sharp liquid rising, climbing and crashing against the white bowl of the toilet, or how the hell I got to the toilet or where the hell I am, shit, I just want to sleep, yeah, sleep and wake up without any dead without any rivers without eyes without voices without.

( )

I didn't know where I was when I woke up. Where, or in whose bed of which room in which hotel of which city. Paloma was asleep next to me with no cover. Her legs lay diagonally, pushing me to one corner of the mattress. Her mouth was half-open and her eyelids were flickering, as if a very faint light had dazzled her in her sleep. I watched her for several minutes, suppressing the desire to ask her about what had gone on in the bar toilet. I could just about recall a few snippets of our journey home, us two staggering our way down a street, perhaps, and so I decided to wake her up. I placed my hand on her shoulder and was surprised to feel the most paper-thin, almost impalpable skin. She didn't move, so I tapped and then shook her a little. Only then did I notice my hands were still numb, the feeling lost in some hidden corner of that bar (parts being erased, subtracted piece by piece).

Felipe was watching us from the foot of the bed looking very serious. He hadn't realised I was awake (or that I could spy on his loner face, his sad face, his grown-up face), but our eyes soon met.

'You little minx!' he cried, winking at me and pointing at Paloma, who also sat up suddenly on the edge of the bed, startled by Felipe's excessive outburst. Felipe began to clap his hands and dish out instructions for how we should tackle the day.

'Come on, girlies, time to get up,' he ordered between claps, while everything around me returned to its place: the sheets, the paintings, Paloma's back unfurling, straightening out, moving away and off towards the bathroom. I also returned to my body, although now it felt all wrong, like an outfit that was too tight around the back. I rubbed my eyes until I'd snapped out of my stupor and only then was I struck by a new sensation. I felt surprisingly fine. I was fine and I was a long way from home.

Felipe paced from one corner of the room to the other, chivvying us along, telling us we should hit the road before it got too late. He knocked on the bathroom door twice and when he finally managed to lure out Paloma – less than impressed and still sleepy, her arms stretched above her head and her hair all matted – he announced that he had a surprise.

'But first let's make a deal, Fräulein. You give me a little bit more of your mother's potion and I'll tell you my little secret.'

Paloma didn't even grace him with eye contact. Instead, she put on yesterday's clothes and sat on the bed looking gaunt. She told Felipe she had one more bottle, just one, a small one she'd rather keep for that night, once we'd found her mum and gone back to Santiago to bury her. She told him it wasn't easy getting hold of that kind of thing, and not to push it. Felipe didn't insist, but the moment Paloma went back to the bathroom he opened her suitcase and began rifling among her socks. Having ruled out several, he eventually found a pair which he shook triumphantly by his ear.

'To keep out the cold,' he said with a wink, and he slipped it into his pocket.

We went down to reception at just past noon. The woman with the black nails interrupted whatever she was doing to wish good luck to Felipe, who just carried on towards the door.

'You must be heading back to Chile today?' she asked, handing me our receipt. I remembered her from the bar, talking to Felipe, dancing with him, whispering in Paloma's ear, and I replied, a little testily, that we still weren't sure; we'd almost certainly be staying in Mendoza for a couple more nights, we weren't in a hurry. She insisted on giving me the receipt and making us pay before we left.

'Isn't today the funeral?' she asked, pointing to the doors. Felipe had stopped in his tracks and from the entrance, visibly upset, he leant his head in and mumbled at me.

'Come here, Iquela, quick, move your arse.'

I went over to him. For a moment I was worried the ground outside would be covered in ash. But there was no ash this time. Instead, I found wreaths of white carnations, freshly picked loose marigolds and daisies festooned all over the roof of the General and on the pavement around it (the flowers like an omen, an amulet).

Paloma pushed her way between us and walked over to the hearse, peering suspiciously through the back window, as if an imposter might be sleeping in the rear compartment. Felipe followed her and together they circled the vehicle; two untrusting animals inspecting the windows and doors for clues.

'Who did all of this?' he asked.

Paloma shrugged her shoulders and stood on her tiptoes to reach a wreath of roses in the middle of the roof. She stretched out her arms, took it and hurled it at the ground. Then she did the same with the remaining hydrangeas and a handful of calla lilies. Thrashing her arms wildly, Paloma gradually cleared the hearse of all the funeral paraphernalia, while Felipe and I looked on, at a loss as to what to do beyond gawping at her increasingly red face. Red with envy. Because it was envy she was feeling; not rage, or sadness or pain. A single phrase betrayed her once we were on the road. Paloma slammed the door shut and her words went on ringing through the hearse.

'This is *my* funeral,' she said. And that was the last we heard from her the whole way.

The engine groaned with the force of the accelerator and the sickly smell of flowers vanished within a few metres. Paloma entertained herself by plucking a daisy that had fallen onto her seat, and she didn't look up from those petals until we were on the motorway. Felipe mumbled instructions to himself as he drove, instructions he debated until he arrived at a private conclusion we weren't privy to, but which translated into a long silence. He kept forgetting to move off at traffic lights and we would be left there, the hearse seemingly stunned before the green light. At no point did I tell him to put his foot down, and I didn't even ask where we were going.

A road sign told me how much further it was to the airport and after a while I let myself be lulled by the distant hum of turbines. After all, it wasn't my mother who'd gone missing, so I wasn't the one disappointing anyone. My own mother was no doubt fine. She had always, in her own way, been fine; she'd learnt how to survive. And her disappointment in me would also be alive and well. It all felt very far away.

We drove up to the security cabin where we'd failed the previous day, and immediately the same guard appeared in his orange overalls and brought down the barrier. Paloma sighed and accused Felipe of making us waste time instead of just going through the established procedures (the proper processes, the regular means, the normal channels). Felipe ignored her and slowed down to a stop right beside the cabin. Everything happened very quickly. The guard poked his head out of the window, surveyed our faces, nodded with satisfaction, and, holding one hand firmly to his temple, saluting the General like a soldier, he raised the barrier and pointed right.

With almost no preamble, as swiftly as the shift from wakefulness to sleep, we found ourselves in the middle of the tarmac, a huge area watched over from afar, on one side, by the immense air traffic control tower. I was surprised by the dimensions of the place and the deafening noise of the turbines, and I asked Paloma to close her window. We drove along a narrow path, parallel to the runway, and headed towards the very edge of the tarmac, where it gave way to a bone-dry plain. There, at the edge of the concrete, lined up like cells, two long rows of hangars appeared before us; great stores housing planes, fuel, spare parts, perhaps. Each hangar was marked with a number on the front. To our right, the even numbers, and in front of us the odds, which is where Felipe headed, muttering a kind of mantra as he went.

'Seven, seven,' he repeated, and the hissing of his 'S's only stopped once we'd parked up.

Felipe jumped out of the car and Paloma and I followed suit. She still seemed resigned or incredulous, and I myself was highly sceptical. He walked ahead of us, in time with that infuriating muttering, and Paloma scurried to catch up with him. Only then, once they were shoulder to shoulder, did her interrogation begin. Paloma wanted to know why that hangar and not another, how did he know, why the airport instead of the consulate. I could hear the anger in her voice and noticed that her cheeks were flaming. Felipe's single-mindedness was driving her mad, as was not knowing where they were heading. Being left out of the search plans infuriated her. It was her funeral, after all. I, on the other hand, didn't even want to know what we were doing there. As far as I knew or cared, her mother might be in one of those hangars, or would show up one day at the morgue in Santiago, or was flying over the Andes at that very moment. She might simply be back in her room in Berlin, or even still at that rally in her white blouse (white, or cream or yellow), locked inside the photograph hanging on the wall of my mother's dining room.

Felipe ignored Paloma's questions and carried on his way, heading up our strange funeral train: a line of mourners led by him, with Paloma huffing and puffing in the middle, and me bringing up the rear, happy to waste all the time in the world (contemplating the *cordillera* in the distance and counting the raw words that I'd left behind).

The doors to hangar number seven were locked with a chain and an enormous padlock. I made one final attempt, more desperate this time. We stopped in front of the lock and I told them it made no sense to go looking in there, that we should do something else, make the most of the trip. I don't even know if they heard me. Felipe took the metal chain with both hands, gave it a tug and the padlock came away without a problem. The doors swung open an inch and all three of us froze before whatever it was that those doors would offer.

Inside, there wasn't a soul to be found, and there were a few signs of neglect that suggested nobody had set foot in there for some time. The air was cold and, despite the place having been totally shut up, it was pleasant, almost refreshing, although I soon felt a vinegary smell waft over me, a sour aftertaste which coated the roof of my mouth (the tubes, the syringes, the dressings). Neither Felipe nor Paloma commented on it. She charged in decisively but soon stopped and became rooted to the spot, as if she'd forgotten what we were there for. Felipe, on the other hand, buried his hands in his pockets, picked himself up and began to stroll about the place with perturbing calm.

It didn't take me long to adjust to the dark. A few rays of sunshine had made it through the hangar doors, but the sheer size of that place meant the light only spread so far as to create a scarcely penetrable darkness. I was surprised by the height of the ceiling, designed to store giant things, not the hundreds of everyday objects that looked even smaller for having been abandoned there. To my left I saw several trolleys of suitcases, bags and rucksacks; mounds of luggage covered in a fine layer of dust (suitcases old and new, hard and soft, bags mounting up in easy, soothing lists). Each trolley had a label on it with the name of an airline, the number of the cancelled flight, its origin and a date. They were all planes that hadn't been able to land in Chile. She couldn't even fully own that tragedy (*her* disaster, *her* funeral, I repeated in my head).

Paloma began to read out the labels on the trolleys, but she wasn't able to get very far. Felipe gave her a pat, almost a caress, on the back.

'We're not going to find your mum here,' he said, 'not unless you put her in a suitcase.'

Paloma abruptly shrugged off that hand and told him she was only looking for the luggage from her mother's flight, to work out if the other suitcases from that flight were there. Even she seemed smaller now, like a little girl as she rummaged through them. Felipe, on the other hand, strutted about the warehouse, as if at last he'd found his true home.

Lined up in a row at the back of the hangar, a dozen containers formed a metal wall. I went over, convinced I'd find the coffin there, but, opening a few, I only found boxes, armchairs, beds, lamps and bicycles; houses dismantled to be put back together somewhere else. You don't ship coffins in those kinds of moves. It made no sense to move country with paintings, cars, clothes and your dead. The idea of finding a coffin there was as ridiculous as finding one adorning a dining room, and it was that image (a decorative coffin, an ornamental coffin) that suddenly seemed funny to me. I stifled a shy giggle but it rang out in that hangar like a church bell. I sensed Paloma's presence behind me. She was following me. As per usual, I was following Felipe, who had paused on the right-hand side of the hangar, and was calling out to me in a broken voice, almost begging me to come.

I could see him standing stock-still with his torso bent forward, his body almost snapped in two (his eyes getting ahead of the rest of him). He went on begging me to come.

'Ique, come and see them, look at them.'

I approached with caution (my pulse climbing up inside my ears: two, four, six seconds wasted in desperation). Every step I took was smaller than the one before; every breath shorter (breathing in the bare minimum). I didn't want to know what Felipe had found. I wasn't ready for it, but I carried on approaching regardless, suppressing my desire to run away and never come back. I stopped beside him and out of the corner of my eye I saw his face, five hundred years older. Paloma came and stood beside me in silence. Our procession line had fallen out of its strict order and we remained like that, overawed like children seeing the sea for the first time, or realising the true magnitude of a death.

There were dozens of them. No. Many more than that. Hundreds of coffins waiting, one on top of the other and stacked together in endless rows, in coffin-lined aisles: an immense labyrinth of floor-to-ceiling plastic coffins, coffins protected in cardboard, small wooden coffins, big wooden coffins, wide and slim, dark and pale. Dozens of perfectly parallel aisles. Hundreds of dead men and women wanting to return, to go back *for good*, to be repatriated (and I tried to make a quick list, an improvised inventory of corpses: fifteen in pine coffins, twenty boxed in chipboard, eight in their poorly varnished caskets).

'Incredible,' Felipe whispered after a long silence. 'Just incredible,' he repeated, and his voice seemed to claw its way up from the deepest part of him, from faraway, from before, from an imprecise and dark place, a dusty voice that had waited patiently to come back and had been kept especially for that moment. A voice identical to the one I'd heard years before.

'Incredible,' he'd said that day as we hid in the blackberry bushes in Chinquihue, on the one and only trip my mother and I made down south, when his Grandma Elsa asked us to go and collect him so he could stay with us that winter; all of a sudden the grief had become too much for her.

'Come quickly and get him.'

He and I were kneeling behind the branches and from there, from down on the ground, we spied on them. His grandma was looking at my mother with her tiny eyes, her eyelids thick like bandages. My mother, on the other hand, wasn't looking at his Grandma Elsa; she was staring towards the sky, as we were. Because what was suspended up there in the air was beyond belief: a little lamb hanging upside down from the branch of an oak tree. A soft, squidgy fruit, just about to break away and fall. Felipe and I looked on, shielded by the blackberries. We watched the blade of the knife slice through the neck of that animal. We watched the blood fall in a sticky stream and then gradually slow into a trickle of thick, shiny drops.

'Incredible,' Felipe said agog, while that mucky white cloud spilt its innards, spewing out a pitcher's worth of red, which filled a saucepan containing coriander and *merquén*.

'Patience,' his Grandma Elsa said to my mother, shaking the pan to spread out the liquid. 'Patience, Consuelo, you have to wait for the blood to congeal, wait a second.'

Because the blood then congealed and changed. It transformed into a different, darker substance, a new material which his grandma cut into soft slices to dissolve in their red mouths.

'Incredible,' Felipe repeated as if he were presiding over a miracle, while I looked at that little animal and then at him, wanting to cover his eyes, to hug him and tell him to close them tight. Felipe, don't look, don't listen, don't say a word, just shut everything, I'm going to be your great-great-great-grandmother and your grandma; I'm going to be your dad. But I found I couldn't promise him anything. All I could do was listen to that word which had returned now, in the hangar.

'Incredible.'

Paloma didn't or perhaps couldn't say a word, but she walked off with intent, as if she'd given herself an order:

move. She took a deep breath, held in the air and made off towards the first row of coffins, as methodical as ever. Felipe started from the second row.

'I can't believe it,' he said. 'They're so tidy, so ordered, Iquela. And there are so, so many of them.' His voice faded into a distant hum and soon they both disappeared.

I drifted in and out of the aisles muttering the same two words, 'Ingrid Aguirre, Ingrid Aguirre,' as if with that name I could fix something irredeemably broken: my father's mistake (Rodolfo's, Víctor's), Ingrid's death (or Elsa's or Claudia's or the deaths of their doubles or aliases), delivering that corpse as if it were an offering that would finally set me free. I inspected every single row keenly, convinced that this was it, my chance to find her and do something important, something vital, something *key*. Something I could own. As if I myself had designed that maze and only I knew how to get out of it, I combed those coffins with extraordinary calm.

I paced up and down those rows like you might browse aisles of books in a vast library, trying to extricate some kind of logic: alphabetical, chronological, thematic (the dead organised by cause of death, ideology, height; corpses classified according to their eagerness to return, or their degree of nostalgia). I wandered among dozens of numbers and names, familiar surnames and unknown origins: Caterina Antonia Baeza Ramos, 1945, Stockholm-Panitao, Jorge Alberto Reyes Astorga, 1951, Montreal-Andacollo, María Belén Sáez Valenzuela, 1939, Caracas-Castro, Juan Camilo García García, 1946, Managua-Valdivia, Miguel, Federica, Elisa, 1963, 1948, 1960, Til-Til, Arica, San Antonio, Curicó, Santiago, Santiago, Santiago.

By the sixth or seventh row, having covered what felt like a hundred countries and every province of Chile, right in the middle of a very long aisle, with two coffins on the bottom row and one propped on top, her name appeared to me: Ingrid Aguirre Azocar, 1953, Berlin-Santiago. I stopped in front of her. The label was written in blue ink and with a careful hand (words that were identical in Spanish and German: mirror-words). The label was stuck carefully to the plastic, and that plastic covered the wood, which held the body which didn't hold anything (or perhaps grief, resentment, boundless nostalgia).

I touched the paper and reread each one of those words (until they dissolved into syllables, and the syllables into letters, and the letters into indecipherable dashes; a blue stain, merely a doodle). I stood there before that piece of paper, a simple label, easily peeled off and slipped inside my pocket, a note that I could erase just like that, prolonging Paloma's search for years, for the rest of her days, in that way offering her a cause. She would never have to go looking for anything else because her fate would be tied to the story of her lost mother (and our parents and all the things they had ever lost). I considered removing that piece of paper and replacing it with another one: any old name and surname, a code name, perhaps (Víctor, Claudia, an arsenal of embodied names). And then I imagined how I would lie to Paloma's face; she would have to go on searching for her mother for the rest of her days, I was so, so sorry. I could effectively bring Paloma's life to a standstill right there and then, erase Ingrid and pick up the telephone straight away, call my mother and tell her that she'd lost her friend for a second time, that I wasn't even capable of doing something as simple as finding her.

I felt a fresh wave of deep unease, as if everything were burning, as if I could no longer sit comfortably in my own skin, as if there were nothing but voices and static and emptiness. Everything that followed was a blur. Not even aware of what I was doing, I withdrew my hand from the label and retreated until my back was resting against the opposite wall of coffins. My two hands formed fists and my nails dug into my palms, and there I stood for a moment, paralysed, unable to piece together a single thought. All the letters of my alphabet were frayed on the floor. Heavy, broken words abandoning me, leaving me terribly alone; alone and with a stupid urge to cry. But instead of crying I took a deep breath, held in that thick air (thick and spent, expired, used up) and let my voice burst out, breaking something inside of me.

'I've found her.'

And I repeated those words lest I start to regret them.

'I've found her.'

He might have told me, the man in the orange overalls, because it's one thing to find a dead body and another to be met by a mountain of stiffs, all in little oblong houses, cos they don't come in graves in the ground any more, they don't store them in cold, clinical boxes, oh no, gone are the dead slung out on pavements and in parks, now they're well and truly bourgeois, and that's better, of course; far better for the dead to be in order, all set to cross the *cordillera* in their troops and have me take them away in handfuls, minus three, minus six, minus nine dead, first to subtract them and then to count each of their bones, yeah, though this number of bones is enough to make my head spin, there are just too many, and it's annoying how many dead have come from Lisbon and Catalonia, and even from Leningrad and Stalingrad, cos they've travelled all the way from the past, but they didn't make it to Chile, no, that's why I'd better slow down and take a deep breath, inhale and hold in the smell and the stillness, embalm the stillness in formaldehyde and only then return over the *cordillera*, with the Grim Reaper himself in tow, that's it, and then, once back in Santiago, in the heart of the ash, I'll pause for a moment, arch my back and exhale all that embalmed stillness, and with each exhalation I'll sink my hands into a hole, a pit that I'm going to dig with my hard nails, cos I'm going to dig till the black earth hides the half-moons on my lunulae, my cuticles, my dog-claw nails, yeah, and with my four hairy paws and my pointy muzzle I'm going to dig, with my filthy claws I'm going to scrape away the ash until I've drawn a horizontal line, a long line that reads 'minus', yeah, and there, in that minus, I'm going to bury them, inter them, lower them carefully down into that bone-dry earth, my bone-dry earth, plant those bones and throw earth over them, cover them in dust and then watch them with my eyes, my hundreds of eyes rapt on seeing that mound of fertile earth, and then, when each one of my dead is in the ground, I'm going to re-dig the same hole and remove the earth to disinter them, exhume them one by one, lick them and hold a vigil for them again, every day and every night for the rest of my life, until there's no ground left unstirred, until even the deserts, the ghost towns, the dirty beaches and apple groves have been ploughed, until I've made up for each one of those missing funerals, that's what I should do, take all those bodies and bury them so at last the figures add up, the bodies and the tombs, the births and the burials, yeah, that's my plan, but then I get distracted, Iquela's talking to me, Iquela's shouting that she's found her, that's what she says, I've found her, and I go over and I can't believe it, cos no one ever finds anything unless they're really looking and Iquela never actually wanted to find dead Ingrid, but all the same she's shouting that she's found her, and only then do I see her; there's a coffin with a little sheet of paper with her name on it, and I close my eyes in horror and touch the wood with my sweaty palm, cos it was meant to be me who found her, Iquela, me, bloody hell, stop sticking your nose in where it's not wanted, because dead Ingrid is mine, mine to

subtract, for fuck's sake, and her wood is smoother than all
the rest, so smooth it makes me sick, yeah, because smooth
things make me sick and the nausea knocks me for six and
I back away and hide to hack up my disgust, I have to get
rid of that rancid smell, that revolting smell of death, so I
shrink behind the other coffins, I slip away to hide from the
German and take out the secret sock, cos I kept this liquid
for me, yeah, to erase me, to dissolve me, and so I shake
it, raise a solitary toast and drink from the little bottle, I
take two wet sips and the liquid slowly kills me, it kills the
smell and the smoothness, it kills the fear and the numbers,
the hate and the envy, and I take another swig and I feel
myself levitating over my body and the German nabs me,
though I can't quite be sure if she's seen me, because I'm
disappearing piece by piece, slipping away and I go back to
Iquela, standing with the famous Ingrid, I walk towards her,
invisible, and I see her pushing the coffin, help me, Felipe,
and I can't understand a word of what she's saying and I'm
dizzy and cold and I don't want warm vomit in my throat
and that's why I stop and hold it in, Felipe I'm talking to you,
help me pull it over to the hearse, and I go over and rest my
hands on the wood and the wood is smooth and I push it,
that's it, with all my animal might I push it but it doesn't
move, no, fuck she's heavy that Ingrid, but I'm strong, yeah,
I push the pain and the wood and the disgust too, I push it
and the coffin at last starts to shift, yeah, and we pull and I
use all my animal strength and I'm grunting and sweating
and hundreds of eyes are watching me, thousands of them
watching me through their wooden boxes, yeah, and you
have your father's eyes, my Gran Elsa says, just like your
father, and it takes all I have to say, no, that's a lie, and it's
my voice speaking and I don't want to hear my damned voice

any more, not one more bloody word from my mouth and that's why I go quiet, cos I've got cow eyes, for fuck's sake, I've got salty squidgy eyes and I don't have the eyes of any father, my eyes are mine, mine, mine, I'm the son of the petals and of my great-great-great-grandmother, and of me, that's what I am, my own son, and with my canine strength at last I drag her along, as if I were trying to cut through the earth, to plough a trench, yeah, and then the coffin falls to the ground with a bang and I catch my breath and push, further and further, and I push her up the ramp on the back of the hearse, all the way onto the rails, the General's rails which should be cold, cos I'm cold and dead Ingrid must be cold though she's now snug in the General, this hearse which has been filled as last, yeah, and I catch my breath and then I watch everything split in two, the whole warehouse splits down the middle, all thanks to the magical curing potion, and Iquela also splits in two, I see her in two pieces and I kiss my hand and blow her a loud, broken kiss, a great-great-great-grandson kiss, that's it, ciao great-great-great-grandma, I call out silently, ciao, I tell her, I love you so much, so so much, and I dash into the hearse and start her up, and the General splutters and shudders, and I can see the German taking photos of all the dead, all these dead I leave behind without a second glance, cos the engine's running and I step on it, I put my foot down because *this* body, dead Ingrid, she's mine, and they can't take that away from me, no, oh no, they can't take that body away from me.

179

( )

It took a while for me to work out what had happened. The metal doors to the hangar were still lashing against the lintel and the hearse was speeding away across the airport tarmac when Paloma took me by the wrist, demanding an explanation.

'I don't believe this,' she said. 'She's mine.'

The General disappeared into the horizon and it didn't take long for Paloma's surprise to turn to rage. It had to be a bad joke, or we were just trying to put the wind up her, or maybe Felipe and I had planned this whole sick game. Her voice sounded strange, childish, like she couldn't control it, and I did my best to explain to her that I understood even less than she did what had just happened. Felipe had gone and this was merely his way of forcing me to catch up with him as soon as possible (to be his witness, his shadow).

An old image of Felipe (a dusty, almost obsolete image) suddenly came back to me, as if I'd buried it years earlier and it had now been dredged up to force me to think about it again: Felipe a few yards from me in the front garden, crouched down in front of the thick bars of the gate that separated us from the road, waving at me to get on my knees next to him, on our marks.

'Ready, Iquela?' he asks in his increasingly hostile voice, a voice that I had tried to forget so as to erase the whole memory (or at least not waste it).

'You ready, Ique?' he asks, slapping me on the back, daring me, goading me for the last time to see if I had it in me, if I was strong enough, if I was sure that I could do it. And I nodded mutely from the ground, my mouth dry, my saliva tangy, my teeth chattering away the fear, anticipating the pain, waiting for the instruction that would launch us into our race.

'On your marks, get set, go! No cheating, Ique! No hands and no standing up. Only on your knees!' Felipe cried, trying to gain ground and already through the gate, ahead of me. Only our knees were allowed to bear the brunt of that trail of rocks he himself had laid out along our race course. Because a few minutes earlier, Felipe had walked the length of the street with his pockets bursting with rocks, scattering them.

'An assault course,' he'd said, while I'd looked on in horror at the little stones strewn along the pavement; tiny shards of glass that glinted in the sun before digging into my skin, step by excruciating step, over and over again. Until finally I was forced to give in, stop and let Felipe speed ahead on his sacrificial race, his pilgrimage, the winner's trophy encrusted in his knees. One lap around the block and then his triumphant return to our finishing line, the door to my mother's house, the woman herself peering down on us from the garden where she was watering the plants, making secret bets with herself as to who would win the race (drowning the lawn, the path, flooding my memory). Felipe arrived back to the house teetering on the edge of laughter and tears, panting, coughing, his nostrils flared and his face dripping with sweat, driven in a terrible state of agitation that only my mother could ease.

'Go inside, Felipe. Dust off that dirt, clean your cuts with salt water, change your clothes and smarten up. It's your turn to choose dinner, whatever you like.' (Felipe had returned, repatriated himself on his knees.)

I'd let myself be carried away by that memory and was surprised to see it was getting dark as we left the hangar. The guard from the security cabin approached us inquisitively, looking for the hearse and trying to gauge with his eyes something he couldn't bring himself to ask. Paloma stormed right up to him and bombarded him with questions. He seemed genuinely upset. Biting his lower lip, he shook his head and, after a long pause in which his eyebrows knitted together in one bushy line, he said he hadn't known. He'd never imagined that the coffin belonged to her mother. He'd assumed that the relative (the child, the bereaved) was the young man. He explained, apologetically, that he'd bumped into Felipe at the bar the night before.

'I was just having a few drinks when this kid staggers out of the bathroom, off his head drunk or high, what do I know, and he comes over looking for a fight. Obviously I thought he was a pain in the arse, but a piss-up beats a bust-up any day, so I offered him a drink.' (A sip, two, the liquid swirling madly.) 'And that's what we were doing when the kid flips out, starts to shake and goes as pale as a ghost telling me that he's lost someone important.'

Paloma glared at him, as if he'd taken something very precious from her.

'Felipe, that was his name,' the guard said, pulling out a pack of cigarettes from the pocket of his overalls. 'The kid had lost someone called Felipe. I couldn't make sense of what he was saying at first, but after a while I knew it had to be someone important,' he went on, lighting a cigarette and taking a deep drag as if all the world's air were contained in its filter. 'Don't think I ever saw a kid that desolate. He was reeling.'

The guard exhaled, hiding his face behind the cloud of smoke.

'He said it had been a horrible death.' (Drowned in the river, hanged from electrical cables, choked on ash.) 'The poor kid was mumbling something about dying being horrible, horrible, and he told me to avoid it at all costs, that no way was he going to die, and that comment seemed a bit odd to me, but the worst thing was what he told me about some empty tombs and some sort of count, or countdown, subtraction, he called it, but then what do I know?' (Nothing, he knew absolutely nothing.)

Paloma listened in silence, her eyes popping out of their sockets. I didn't interrupt him either. A plane flew overhead, towards an imprecise point in the sky, and the guard filled the time it took for that din to fade by offering Paloma a cigarette.

'It's my last one, sorry,' he said to me, striking a match to light it.

They smoked in sync, an excruciating break in the story's action, a pause filled only by the blast of turbines. And then the guard picked up where he'd left off.

'That's why I left the hangar unlocked. I told the kid about those coffins and I told him he could find them in number seven,' he said, pointing back to the doors. 'Long story short, he was going to do me a favour in return. The thing is, those coffins have been left there for days. It looked like no one was coming to claim them, and us lot working here are stuck with the stench, this stench of shit, pardon the expression,' he added to Paloma, flaring his nostrils. 'It's stomach-turning and I don't know what to do. The powers that be don't know what to do. No one seems to want to claim responsibility for them. I mean, what are we meant to do with all those bodies?'

The man dropped his cigarette, stubbed it out with his shoe and, without taking his eyes off the ground (the glowing tip now mere ash), he asked Paloma to forgive him.

'It never occurred to me that it wasn't the kid's coffin. Who would go around like that, like a crazy person, looking for someone else's corpse? Although, I suppose, what does it matter whose dead they are, right? That's not the issue,' he went on, frowning. 'No, the issue is something else entirely,' he added, now more sure of himself. 'When it comes to the dead we've got to help each other out. There are just too many of them.'

The guard headed in the direction of the hangar, took the metal chain, locked the doors and reluctantly offered to drive us back into town. He said that in Mendoza we could rent a car to get back to Santiago and that with any luck we'd catch up with Felipe along the way; that's all he could do for us, the rest fell outside his remit (or really, the remains did). Without consulting me, Paloma accepted his offer. I had nothing to add, in any case. I was distracted by another plane taking off and the invasive echo of my thoughts. Maybe we should do something about all those coffins; maybe each one of those piled-up caskets and the endless list of names and surnames – the whole hangar, even – was somehow also mine (like the ash and the unavoidable *cordillera*).

I gazed up at the setting sun, at a complete loss as to what to say. And there, standing before the runway, imagining that never-ending road, as drawn out as our search had been, I foresaw everything that was going to happen: just like before, the two trails of blood emblazoned on the pavement marking out the least painful route, the one Felipe had already cleared; just like before, my body collapsing to my knees and my mother's disappointment boring into my back; and just like before, Felipe dragging himself towards her, his knees grazed and filthy like two bloody badges of honour.

I was sure that all I had to do to earn that look from her (that glinting knife-edge of a look, 'now clean up your cuts with salt water') was to get down on the ground and crawl on my hands and knees to the guard's van, sit between him and Paloma and lead us home with the map.

As if something were forcing me to get to the end of that old memory, of that race lost from the starting line, or as if it were my duty to fill in the holes in it, each detail of my homecoming appeared then in crystal clear sequence, opening up a chasm into the past (a slip, a typo). I pictured myself going back along that mountain road, taking days, weeks to scale those peaks on my knees, making my way through all those mountain chains and the thick curtains of ash, determined to reach my goal. I pictured the leaden light dimming the skies, the curves and crags of Los Penitentes, the vineyards obliterated by all the grey, and the fields caked in dust. And I saw myself entering the city, back in my city at last, my eyes looking up at the ash which would still be falling, that terrible powder plastered over parks and homes, burying everything I'd ever known beneath its blanket of crushed stone (cities shrouded in white sheets). And once there, I would look for traces of Felipe in the horrendous stillness of the footprints. And following the deepest tracks, having wandered lost for hours, I would find him, the hearse parked sidelong across the Alameda, and inside, as still as a statue, Felipe lying face up, waiting. And I would walk over to talk to him and tell him to come with me, to forget about everything, absolutely everything, but something strange would hit me then. As if I'd never met him, as if that man lying on his back in the hearse were completely unrelated to Felipe, as if he were embodying another man altogether, Felipe would appear before me as a perfect stranger, as a vaguely familiar face accompanying a coffin, his meek hands lying across his chest (a chest covered in words like 'hollow', 'niche', 'extinguished'). And only then, from the middle of the street, in the wake of that missed encounter, would I sit behind the wheel of the General and dare to look one last time at the watchful *cordillera*. And I would see words like that, like 'watchful', discarded along the mountain road. From there I would see each phrase abandoned along the way. Words like 'decisive' and 'arsenal' would be left up there at the summit; abandoned words like 'rails' and 'scar' (and 'howl' and 'tear' and 'splinter'). Because only by ridding myself of it all would I be able to face going back; only by shaking off the 'scars', 'grief', 'sorrows', and repaying, syllable by syllable, that incalculable debt, a debt that would have rendered us mute. Exhausted and nervous, I would drive right up to those iron gates and find the lawn flooded in dirty water (the water rotting words and letters, a whole language drowned). I would park up the hearse in front of the door and right there, blocking the gate to the house (on our marks, under the threshold of our finish line) I would leave that black, rectangular offering in the front garden where my mother would be watering the plants. Because I'd find my mother there, always with that hose, and I'd look at her for a moment (her feet buried in that mire with its smell of old earth; old, but mine). And I would creep towards her without making a sound ('because we mustn't make a sound'), very carefully ('because we've good reason to be afraid, my girl. Always prepare for the worst'). I'd walk towards my mother, gazing at her affectionately, carrying the weight of all the things she'd ever seen (carrying remains, debts, sorrows). And in an old voice – no less mine for being inherited – using frail and untranslatable syllables, final words which, once spoken, would leave me empty and alone in a desert full of new lines (to be spoken in a timeless language), I would say to her with a hint of sadness, 'I've brought you Ingrid Aguirre, and here is Felipe Arrabal.' And I would hold her (her skin so close to her bones and her bones so close to mine), and only then, from within that perfect parenthesis of our interwoven bodies, would I open my mouth to tell her:

'Mother, I've done all this for you.'

I felt a wave of dizziness, as if all the air in my body had suddenly left me and I were tumbling into the void. A horn honked a few metres away where the guard was waiting, waving at us from inside a van. Paloma was telling me to get a move on, they were waiting for us, there was no time to waste. And behind her, beyond the tarmac, lighting up the edges of an untouched landscape, a purple sun disappeared behind the mountains: not drowning in the sea, but tucking itself back down behind the *cordillera* where it came from.

Paloma made off towards the guard but then stopped, walked back, took my hand and said she wouldn't know where to start looking on her own.

'Iquela, come on, please.'

The horn fell silent and in that pause I heard a murmur in the red sky, the wind rustling the branches of a faraway forest. Paloma did her best to persuade me to go with her, to get in that van and together cross the mountains, to find the other two, wherever they were. She was growing increasingly exasperated. As she spoke (from afar, and moving further and further away) I noticed, in the near distance, dozens of birds preparing for flight, their wings blazing in the glow of the van headlights.

I shook my head from side to side, making my refusal clear as I calculated the distance between us and those birds. And I heard myself speaking calmly, decisively (a new voice, a newly born voice).

'I'll see you later,' I told Paloma with a kiss. 'I'll catch you up,' I added, pulling her in for a hug, remembering our first encounter (wondering if it was a new kind of longing beating inside of me, or if it was still the steady pulse of our parents' nostalgia).

Paloma got into the van and waved me goodbye. And I watched as she drove away, leaving only those wings beating in steady unison before me, the perfect harmony of birds in flight, taking off to the sound of a strange lullaby, a murmur that burst suddenly into an uncontainable din.

0

And I step on it so I don't get stuck in that squidgy tar, that grey mud, in that pus, that's it, so I'm not swallowed up by the pus oozing out the mountains, the *cordillera* whispering at me to go on, put your foot down, get your motor runnin', we sang, that time we sang our hearts out, Iquela and I, so that we didn't have to listen, so that we couldn't hear a word, the mountain goading me now to climb higher, to keep going, forget about the twenty, fifteen, ten kilometres per hour choking the General; but this isn't proving so easy, no, it's no joke getting him up the grey *cordillera*, but I keep driving anyway, we keep climbing, and I'm sweating so I open the windows to let a little air in, despite all the pus on the other side I wind down the hearse windows, and that damn pus rushes in like a wave, in and up my sleeves, yeah, and it sticks to my skin this poison, this virus that wants to infect my eyes, and that's why I start crying grey tears, to wash clean my skin, and then the pus and my tears mix together and I'm completely drenched in ash, and something happens, the General shudders and shakes, shush, easy now, let's see, nice and slow, back into neutral, but he chokes, come on now, let's just roll down here, but he coughs, moans and refuses to go, no, the General won't go up the hill, bloody hell, the hearse breaks down, there's no persuading him, he kicks the bucket and I'm left with no choice but to get out, and only then, as I plant my feet on the ground, do I notice what a hole I'm in: it's the summit to end all summits, the peak, the grey zenith, this is where the General came to die, he's burnt out and silent now, shush, rest in peace, and I listen to his death rattle, one final howl, and there's a thick fug of exhaust fumes surrounding him, drowning him, separating me from her too, because she, Ingrid Aguirre, Berlin-Smokepall, is also disappearing in the smoke, and then, as rigorous as ever with my calculations, I subtract her, that's right, minus one, I write it down, minus one, I bawl, minus one, minus one, but it's not enough! I subtract her but I don't get to zero, bloody hell! the German's mum can't have been mine to subtract, just some generic stiff, an impostor, a fake, yeah, and that's when I fall to my knees, defeated, and I look at it, a smoked-out mausoleum in the mountains, a cliff-edge coffin, a crypt-cum-*cordillera*, and I can't believe this is happening, so I take another sip of that white liquid, a big gulp to erase myself, to numb the feeling of this sorrow spreading through me, forcing me to look down at my own skin, my new skin which isn't dark like before, because when I look down I see my legs are no longer legs, my arms are no longer arms, and gone are the elbows, the fingers, the wrists, now I'm covered in scales, no, something else, my skin is shiny but dry, there are feathers tacked to my skin, feathers to protect me, to set me apart, to mark me out from the rest, and nor are my eyes my eyes, they're dry and pale, broken shards of glass, yeah, and soon with my broken eyes I realise how light I am, with my shattered pupils I see my winged body and there below, the city, completely still, the city like a deep round nest, circular like navels, like night-time thoughts, that's Santiago, a round nest, just like my flight home on this round trip, cos I think I'd better forget about the General now and fly back to the city, fly back home, return, that's it, and that's what gets me up on my feet, what makes me turn my back on that devious stiff in her fug, and I dust myself off and walk away from all that, from her, from myself, and I run, I run to see how these wings of mine work, I flap them with all my might to unfold them, to build up their strength, but I can't, no, they're so heavy these beginner's wings, wings of stone, bloody good-for-nothing wings were all I needed, but all the same I run for hours, and evening falls, then night falls and I go on beating my wings in the dark, I keep trying all through the black night until the darkness lifts and the dawn meets me flapping my wings, and with the dawn I leave those mortuary mountains behind, descend the last of those eastern hills, and before I know it I'm in Santiago, a new Santiago, one which seems to be warning me, watching me, trapping me, yeah, and for a while I get lost among its narrow streets, but at last I come out on the Alameda, the broad Alameda, and I stop dead in my tracks, cos I've finally worked it out: this avenue is my clue, this concrete road is the way, not the airport, not Mendoza, but this deserted Alameda, and so I catch my breath, one, two, three seconds, I look over at the bridge, four, five, I drink what's left of the white liquid, six, seven, I shudder and take a deep breath, eight, my chest swells, nine, I gather momentum, ten, and I run down the Alameda like I've never run in my life, like you only run for the last time, I pound down the middle of the road leaving buildings and monuments in my wake, leaving Saint Lucía, the Moneda and the waterless fountains behind me, I run through the centre like long-legged birds run, the ones who take off all slow and heavy, and my sad pups follow me, my orphans yowling their goodbyes, and I go on flapping my trembling wings, running till my feet come off the ground, till I take off, lift off, yeah! higher, higher, higher, and my wings are braced and the concrete comes away beneath my claws and my legs retract as if they knew, as if my legs remembered that they have to become more streamlined, and I feel my chest filling with the finest air, a light air that lifts me up like helium, and I catch a current and my claws retract and my spine extends and I'm so light, yeah, finally, with the dawn, my wings have woken up, that's it, I'm flying, yeah, I'm flying with my wings outstretched, wings so wide I can't see the edges of my own body, the edges of my arms which are beating so serenely, so beautifully, and the wind whistles against my body and I sigh a happy sigh as I soar, swerving gently with each puff of this air cocooning me, cos it's swaddling me, Santiago's air, the sky falls in on itself to touch me, it crumbles into ash and the ash sings to me, sings me a lullaby, and what I really want is to fly away forever, fly higher and higher until I disappear and I'm nothing but a shadow, that's why I climb so high, far from the deserted Alameda, and my pups fade into the distance, and so too do the tree tops and the Pío Nono Bridge and the clock of stopped time and the meadowlarks, they fade with my pups, and with them the pigeons and the sad street rats, and my lonely flowers are left all on their own, like all the lonely parents and all the lonely children, because I keep climbing till I can't see anything but the distant course of the Mapocho, that bend I know as if it were my own body, cos the basin is buried under my skin, in the lines on the palm of my hand; my blood runs through the city, this city which is my body, it's my nest, my zero, yeah, and then, from all the way up in the sky's shell I feel a tingling, a fever, an overwhelming sadness that makes me shut my eyes, because I can feel those black thoughts pulling me back down to earth, dragging me, calling me, and the vertigo sends me into a tailspin and I plummet down towards the sky; my body falls away from me and the pain falls away, the air tumbles out of me and my tired wings fall away too as I watch my shadow grow steadily bigger on the ground, a sharp shadow, which means there must also be a light, a light shining right through my face and dazzling the pupils in my pores and illuminating my descent, my blazing collapse, my very own fire, yeah, because I am the fire, a fire with the wings of a plummeting sun, that's it, and in my fear and with this urgency I watch as the fire spills out of me and all over Santiago, spills onto that grey tarmac beneath my wasted body, and I sink my claws into my nest, into the very centre of this square, I curl up on the ground and bury myself in what's left, among the remains, in the barren dryness of this ash, of these ashes, and with my last breath I open my eyes to face the lightning flash, to face the beam lighting up Santiago and the sky, this open, deep blue sky, blue-blue, yeah, the blue of the fire burning everything, because all the cobbles and the walls and the shops are ablaze, the buildings and the poplars are aflame, the petals and the sepals and the corollas are burning, each thing and all its parts are burning, the whole of Santiago is on fire and I shine in the light of those flames, because I am the fire and the ash, the most perfect, golden bird, that's why I have to do it, like a circle must be perfect I have to say the words, to sing my furious song in my radiant voice, in a voice that dies and is reborn I have to scream as I blaze, as I give birth to myself, as the flames give life to me I have to scorch the air with my voice, with my final howl, my final sum, minus one, minus one, minus one.

Dear readers,

As well as relying on bookshop sales, And Other Stories relies on subscriptions from people like you for many of our books, whose stories other publishers often consider too risky to take on.

Our subscribers don't just make the books physically happen. They also help us approach booksellers, because we can demonstrate that our books already have readers and fans. And they give us the security to publish in line with our values, which are collaborative, imaginative and 'shamelessly literary'.

All of our subscribers:

- receive a first-edition copy of each of the books they subscribe to
- are thanked by name at the end of our subscriber-supported books
- receive little extras from us by way of thank you, for example: postcards created by our authors

BECOME A SUBSCRIBER, OR GIVE A SUBSCRIPTION TO A FRIEND

Visit andotherstories.org/subscriptions/ to help make our books happen. You can subscribe to books we're in the process of making. To purchase books we have already published, we urge you to support your local or favourite bookshop and order directly from them – the often unsung heroes of publishing.

OTHER WAYS TO GET INVOLVED

If you'd like to know about upcoming events and reading groups (our foreign-language reading groups help us choose books to publish, for example) you can:

- join our mailing list at: andotherstories.org
- follow us on Twitter: @andothertweets
- join us on Facebook: facebook.com/AndOtherStoriesBooks
- admire our books on Instagram: @andotherpics

This book was made possible thanks to the support of:

Aaron McEnery · Aaron Peck · Aaron Schneider · Ada Gokay · Adam Bowman · Adam Butler · Adam Lenson · Adriana Diaz Enciso · Agata Rucinska · Aileen-Elizabeth Taylor · Ailsa Peate · Aisling Reina · Ajay Sharma · Alan Donnelly · Alan Reid · Alana Marquis-Farncombe · Alastair Gillespie · Alastair Laing · Alex Fleming · Alex Hancock · Alex Ramsey · Alexandra de Verseg-Roesch · Alexandra Stewart · Alexia Richardson · Ali Smith · Alice Toulmin · Alison Riley · Alison Winston · Alyse Ceirante · Amanda · Amber Da · Amelia Dowe · Amy Benson · Amy Rushton · Amy Slack · Anastasia Carver · Andra Dusu · Andrea Reece · Andrew Lees · Andrew Marston · Andrew McCallum · Andrew Reece · Andrew Rego · Angus Walker · Ann Moore · Ann Sheasby · Anna Badkhen · Anna Milsom · Anna Pigott · Anne Carus · Anne Guest · Anne Kangley · Anne Ryden · Anne Sanders · Annette Hamilton · Annie McDermott · Annie Syed · Anonymous · Anonymous · Anonymous · Anonymous · Antonia Lloyd-Jones · Antonio de Swift · Antony Pearce · Aoife Boyd · Archie Davies · Arne Van Petegem · Asako

Serizawa · Asher Norris · Ashley Callaghan · Audrey Mash · Avril Marren · Barbara Black · Barbara Mellor · Barbara Wheatley · Ben Schofield · Ben Thornton · Benedict Durrant · Benjamin Judge · Beth Sarmiento · Beverly Jackson · Bianca Jackson · Bianca Winter · Björn Halldórsson · Brendan McIntyre · Briallen Hopper · Brian Byrne · Bridget Gill · Bridget Starling · Brigita Ptackova · Caitlin Halpern · Caitlin Liebenberg · Caitriona Lally · Cameron Lindo · Caren Harple · Carla Carpenter · Carlos Gonzalez · Carol Christie · Carol-Ann Davids & Micah Naidoo · Carolina Pineiro · Caroline Bennett · Caroline Mager · Caroline Picard · Caroline Waight · Caroline West · Carolyn Johnson · Cassidy Hughes · Catherine Barton · Catherine Lambert · Catherine Taylor · Cathy Czauderna · Catriona Gibbs · Cecilia Rossi · Cecilia Uribe · Cecily Maude · Chantal Wright · Charles Fernyhough · Charles Raby · Charles Wolfe · Charles Dee Mitchell · Charlotte Briggs · Charlotte Holtam · Charlotte Murrie & Stephen Charles · Charlotte Whittle · China Miéville · Chris

Belden · Chris Holmes · Chris Hughes · Chris Lintott · Chris McCann · Chris Nielsen · Chris Stevenson · Chris Young · Chris & Kathleen Repper-Day · Christina Harris · Christina Moutsou · Christine Bartels · Christine Dyer · Christine Elliott · Christine Hudnall · Christine Luker · Christopher Allen · Christopher Stout · Ciara Ní Riain · Claire Adams · Claire Brooksby · Claire Malcolm · Claire Tristram · Claire Williams · Claire Wood · Clare Archibald · Clare Young · Clarice Borges · Claudia Hoare · Claudia Nannini · Clive Bellingham · Clive Hewat · Cody Copeland · Colin Denyer · Colin Matthews · Colin Prendergast · Corey Nelson · Courtney Lilly · Craig Barney · Cyrus Massoudi · Dag Bennett · Dan Raphael · Dana Behrman · Daniel Arnold · Daniel Bennett · Daniel Douglas · Daniel Gillespie · Daniel Hahn · Daniel Manning · Daniel Reid · Daniel Sparling · Daniel Sweeney · Daniel Venn · Daniela Steierberg · Darcy Hurford · Darius Cuplinskas · Dave Lander · Dave Young · Davi Rocha · David Anderson · David Hebblethwaite · David Higgins · David Johnson-Davies ·

David F Long · David Mantero · David Shriver · David Smith · David Steege · David Travis · Dean Taucher · Debbie Pinfold · Declan O'Driscoll · Deirdre Nic Mhathuna · Denis Larose · Denis Stillewagt & Anca Fronescu · Denise Muir · Diana Fox Carney · Diana Powell · Dominick Santa Cattarina · Donald Wilson · Duncan Clubb · Duncan Marks · Eamon Flack · Ed Owles · Edward Rathke · Edward Thornton · Ekaterina Beliakova · Elaine Kennedy · Elaine Rassaby · Eleanor Dawson · Eleanor Maier · Elhum Shakerifar · Elie Howe · Elina Zicmane · Elisabeth Cook · Eliza Apperly · Eliza Mood · Eliza O'Toole · Elizabeth Draper · Elizabeth Farnsworth · Elizabeth Stewart · Ellen Coopersmith · Ellen Kennedy · Ellen Wilkinson · Ellie Goddard · Emily Bromfield · Emily Howe · Emily Paine · Emily Taylor · Emily Williams · Emily Yaewon Lee & Gregory Limpens · Emma Bielecki · Emma Louise Grove · Emma Perry · Emma Pope · Emma Strong · Emma Timpany · Enrico Cioni · Erin Cameron Allen · Ewan Tant · F Gary Knapp · Fabienne Berionni · Fatima Kried · Fawzia Kane · Filiz Emre-Cooke · Finbarr Farragher · Fiona Marquis · Fiona Mozley · Florence Reynolds ·

Florian Duijsens · Fran Sanderson · Frances de Pontes Peebles · Francesca Brooks · Francis Mathias · Francisco Vilhena · Franco Vassallo · Frank van Orsouw · Friederike Knabe · Gabriela Lucia Garza de Linde · Gabrielle Crockatt · Gary Gorton · Gavin Collins · Gavin Smith · Gawain Espley · Gaynor Clark · Genaro Palomo Jr · Genia Ogrenchuk · Geoff Thrower · Geoffrey Cohen · Geoffrey Urland · George Christie · George Stanbury · George Wilkinson · Gill Boag-Munroe · Gillian Ackroyd · Gillian Grant · Gillian Spencer · Gordon Cameron · Graham R Foster · Graham Fulcher · Grant Hartwell · Grant Rintoul · Greg Bowman · Gregory Ford · GRJ Beaton · Gwyn Lewis · Hadil Balzan · Hank Pryor · Hannah Lynn · Hans Krensler · Hans Lazda · Hayley Newman · Heather Tipon · Helen Asquith · Helen Brady · Helen Conford · Helen Coombes · Helen Gough · Helen Waland · Helen Wormald · Henrike Laehnemann · Henry Patino · HL Turner-Heffer · Howard Robinson · Hugh Gilmore · Hyoung-Won Park · Ian Barnett · Ian Buchan · Ian Docherty · Ian McMillan · Ian Mond · Ian Randall · Ieva Panavaite & Mariusz Hubski · Ingrid Olsen · Irene Mansfield · Irina Tzanova · Isabel

Adey · Isabella Garment · Isabella Weibrecht · Ivona Wolff · J Collins · Jacinta Perez Gavilan Torres · Jack Brown · Jacqueline Haskell · Jacqueline Lademann · Jacqueline Ting Lin · James Attlee · James Beck · James Crossley · James Cubbon · James Kinsley · James Lehmann · James Lesniak · James Portlock · James Purdon · James Scudamore · James Tierney · Jamie Cox · Jamie Mollart · Jamie Stewart · Jamie Walsh · Jane Leuchter · Jane Rawson · Jane Roberts · Jane Williams · Jane Woollard · Janet Gilmore · Janette Ryan · Jasmine Gideon · Jean-Jacques Regouffre · Jeanne Guyon · Jeehan Quijano · Jeff Collins · Jenifer Logie · Jennifer Arnold · Jennifer Bernstein · Jennifer Petersen · Jenny Huth · Jenny Newton · Jenny Nicholls · Jenny Wilkinson · Jeremy Trombley · Jess Howard-Armitage · Jesse Coleman · Jessica Billington · Jessica Laine · Jessica Loveland · Jessica Martin · Jethro Soutar · Jill Twist · Jillian Jones · Jo Goodall · Jo Harding · Jo Lateu · Joanna Flower · Joanna Luloff · Joanne Badger · Joao Pedro Bragatti Winckler · JoDee Brandon · Jodie Adams · Jodie Martire · Johanna Anderson · Johannes Holmqvist · Johannes Georg Zipp · John Carnahan · John

Conway · John Coyne · John Down · John Gent · John Hartley · John Hodgson · John Kelly · John McKee · John Royley · John Shaw · John Steigerwald · John Winkelman · Jon Talbot · Jonathan Blaney · Jonathan Huston · Jonathan Kiehlmann · Jonathan Ruppin · Jonathan Watkiss · Joseph Camilleri · Joseph Cooney · Joseph Schreiber · Joshua Davis · Judith Virginia Moffatt · Judyth Emanuel · Julia Rochester · Julian Duplain · Julie Gibson · Julius Roberts · Justine Mooney · K Elkes · Kaarina Hollo · Kapka Kassabova · Kara Kogler Baptista · Karen Jones · Karen Waloschek · Karl Chwe · Karl Kleinknecht & Monika Motylinska · Kasim Husain · Kasper Haakansson · Kasper Hartmann · Kate Attwooll · Kate Griffin · Kate Mc Caughley · Katharina Herzberger · Katharine Freeman · Katharine Robbins · Katherine El-Salahi · Katherine Mackinnon · Katherine Sotejeff-Wilson · Kathryn Cave · Kathryn Edwards · Kathryn Kasimor · Kathryn Williams · Katie Brown · Katie Lewin · Katrina Thomas · Keith Walker · Kenneth Blythe · Kerry Young · Kevin Maxwell · Kieron James · Kim Gormley · Kirsten Major · Kirsty Doole · KL Ee · Klara Rešetič · Kris Ann Trimis · Kristina Rudinskas · Krystine

Phelps · Kuaam Animashaun · Lana Selby · Lander Hawes · Lara Vergnaud · Larraine Gooch · Laura Batatota · Laura Clarke · Laura Lea · Laurence Laluyaux · Laurie Sheck & Jim Peck · Leah Cooper · Leah Good · Leanne Radojkovich · Leon Frey · Leonie Schwab · Leonie Smith · Leri Price · Lesley Lawn · Lesley Watters · Liam Buell · Liam Elward · Liliana Lobato · Lily Dunn · Lindsay Brammer · Lindy van Rooyen · Lisa Brownstone · Liz Clifford · Lizzie Broadbent · LJ Nicolson · Loretta Platts · Lorna Bleach · Lorna Scott Fox · Lottie Smith · Louise Foster · Louise Smith · Louise Thompson · Luc Verstraete · Lucia Rotheray · Lucy Goy · Lucy Hariades · Lucy Huggett · Lucy Moffatt · Lucy Wheeler · Luise von Flotow · Luke Healey · Luke Williamson · Lynda Edwardes-Evans · Lynda Graham · Lynn Martin · Lysann Church · M Manfre · Madeleine Kleinwort · Madeline Teevan · Maeve Lambe · Maggie Livesey · Mandy Wight · Marcus Joy · Maria Hill · Marie Donnelly · Marike Dokter · Marina Castledine · Mario Cianci · Mario Sifuentez · Marja S Laaksonen · Mark Sargent · Mark Sztyber · Mark Waters · Martha Nicholson · Martha Stevns · Martin Brown ·

Martin Price · Martin Vosyka · Martin Whelton · Mary Byrne · Mary Carozza · Mary Heiss · Mary Wang · Mary Ellen Nagle · Matt O'Connor · Matt Sosnow · Matt & Owen Davies · Matthew Adamson · Matthew Armstrong · Matthew Banash · Matthew Black · Matthew Francis · Matthew Geden · Matthew Hamblin · Matthew Lowe · Matthew Smith · Matthew Thomas · Matthew Warshauer · Matthew Woodman · Matty Ross · Maureen Freely · Maureen Pritchard · Max Garrone · Max Longman · Meaghan Delahunt · Megan Taylor · Megan Wittling · Meike Ziervogel · Melissa Beck · Melissa Danny · Melissa Quignon-Finch · Meredith Jones · Mette Kongsted · Michael Aguilar · Michael Bichko · Michael James Eastwood · Michael Gavin · Michael McCaughley · Michelle Falkoff · Michelle Lotherington · Mike Bittner · Mike Timms · Mike Turner · Miranda Persaud · Miriam McBride · Mitchell Albert · Monika Olsen · Morgan Bruce · Morven Dooner · Myles Nolan · N Tsolak · Namita Chakrabarty · Nancy Cooley · Nancy Oakes · Nathalie Adams · Nathalie Atkinson · Neil George · Neil Pretty · Nicholas Brown · Nicholas Jowett · Nick James ·

Nick Nelson & Rachel Eley · Nick Sidwell · Nick Twemlow · Nicola Hart · Nicola Sandiford · Nicole Matteini · Nigel Palmer · Nikolaj Ramsdal Nielsen · Nikos Lykouras · Nina Alexandersen · Nina Moore · Ohan Hominis · Olga Brawanska · Olivia Payne · Olivia Tweed · Orla Foster · Pamela Stackhouse · Pashmina Murthy · Pat Winslow · Patricia Sterritt · Patricia Webbs · Patrick McGuinness · Paul Cray · Paul Jones · Paul Munday · Paul Robinson · Paula Edwards · Paula McGrath · Penelope Hewett Brown · Penny East · Penny Schofield · Penny Simpson · Peter Goulborn · Peter McBain · Peter McCambridge · Peter Rowland · Peter Vos · Peter Wells · Philip Carter · Philip Lom · Philip Warren · Philipp Jarke · Philippa Hall · Piet Van Bockstal · PM Goodman · PRAH Foundation · Rachael Williams · Rachel Gregory · Rachel Jones · Rachel Lasserson · Rachel Matheson · Rachel Van Riel · Rachel Watkins · Raeanne Lambert · Ralph Cowling · Rebecca Braun · Rebecca Moss · Rebecca Roadman · Rebecca Rosenthal · Rebekah Hughes · Renee Humphrey · Rhiannon Armstrong · Rhodri Jones · Richard Ashcroft · Richard Bauer · Richard Clifford · Richard Gwyn · Richard Mansell · Richard McClelland · Richard Priest · Richard Shea · Richard Soundy · Rishi Dastidar · RM Foord · Robert Collinson · Robert Gillett · Robert Hannah · Robert Hugh-Jones · Robin Graham · Robin Taylor · Roger Newton · Ronnie Friedland · Rory Dunlop · Rory Williamson · Rosalind May · Rosalind Ramsay · Rosalind Sanders · Rosanna Foster · Rose Crichton · Ross Scott & Jimmy Gilmore · Ross Trenzinger · Roxanne O'Del Ablett · Roz Simpson · Rozzi Hufton · Ruchama Johnston-Bloom · Rupert Ziziros · Ryan Grossman · S Italiano · Sabrina Uswak · Sajeda Mulla · Sally Baker · Sally Thomson · Sam Gordon · Sam Reese · Sam Ruddock · Samantha Murphy · Samantha Smith · Samuel Daly · Sandra Mayer · Sara Di Girolamo · Sarah Arboleda · Sarah Boyce · Sarah Costello · Sarah Duguid · Sarah Harwood · Sarah Lucas · Sarah Pybus · Sarah Smith · Sarah Strugnell · Sarah Watkins · Sasha Bear · Sasha Dugdale · Satara Lazar · Scott Thorough · Sean Malone · Sejal Shah · Seonad Plowman · Sez Kiss · SH Makdisi · Shannon Beckner · Shannon Knapp · Shauna Gilligan · Sheridan Marshall · Sherman Alexie · Shira Lob · Sigurjon Sigurdsson · Simon Pitney · Simon Robertson · Sindre Bjugn · SJ Bradley · SK Grout · Sofia Mostaghimi · Sonia Pelletreau · Sophie Goldsworthy · ST Dabbagh · Stacy Rodgers · Stefanie May IV · Stefano Mula · Stephan Eggum · Stephanie Lacava · Stephen Pearsall · Steve Chapman · Steven Williams · Steven & Gitte Evans · Stuart Wilkinson · Subhasree Basu · Sue & Ed Aldred · Susan Allen · Susan Benthall · Susan Ferguson · Susan Higson · Susan Irvine · Susan Manser · Susanna Fidoe · Susie Roberson · Suzanne Lee · Tamar Shlaim · Tamara Larsen · Tammy Watchorn · Tamsin Dewé · Tania Hershman · Tanja Heilbronner · Teresa Griffiths · Terry Kurgan · Tessa Lang · The Mighty Douche Softball Team · Thomas Baker · Thomas Bell · Thomas Chadwick · Thomas Fritz · Thomas Legendre · Thomas Mitchell · Thomas Rowley · Thomas van den Bout · Tiffany Lehr · Tiffany Stewart · Tim Hopkins · Tim & Pavlina Morgan · Tim Theroux · Timothy Nixon · Tina Rotherham-Winqvist · Toby Day · Toby Halsey · Tom Atkins · Tom Darby · Tom Dixon · Tom Franklin · Tom Gray · Tom Lake · Tom Stafford · Tom Whatmore · Tom Wilbey · Tony Bastow · Tony Messenger · Torna

Current & Upcoming Books

01 Juan Pablo Villalobos, *Down the Rabbit Hole*
translated from the Spanish by Rosalind Harvey

02 Clemens Meyer, *All the Lights*
translated from the German by Katy Derbyshire

03 Deborah Levy, *Swimming Home*

04 Iosi Havilio, *Open Door*
translated from the Spanish by Beth Fowler

05 Oleg Zaionchkovsky, *Happiness is Possible*
translated from the Russian by Andrew Bromfield

06 Carlos Gamerro, *The Islands*
translated from the Spanish by Ian Barnett

07 Christoph Simon, *Zbinden's Progress*
translated from the German by Donal McLaughlin

08 Helen DeWitt, *Lightning Rods*

09 Deborah Levy, *Black Vodka: ten stories*

10 Oleg Pavlov, *Captain of the Steppe*
translated from the Russian by Ian Appleby

11 Rodrigo de Souza Leão, *All Dogs are Blue*
translated from the Portuguese by Zoë Perry & Stefan Tobler

12 Juan Pablo Villalobos, *Quesadillas*
translated from the Spanish by Rosalind Harvey

13 Iosi Havilio, *Paradises*
translated from the Spanish by Beth Fowler

14 Ivan Vladislavić, *Double Negative*

15 Benjamin Lytal, *A Map of Tulsa*

16 Ivan Vladislavić, *The Restless Supermarket*

17 Elvira Dones, *Sworn Virgin*
translated from the Italian by Clarissa Botsford

18 Oleg Pavlov, *The Matiushin Case*
translated from the Russian by Andrew Bromfield

19 Paulo Scott, *Nowhere People*
translated from the Portuguese by Daniel Hahn

20 Deborah Levy, *An Amorous Discourse in the Suburbs of Hell*

21 Juan Tomás Ávila Laurel, *By Night the Mountain Burns*
translated from the Spanish by Jethro Soutar

22 SJ Naudé, *The Alphabet of Birds*
translated from the Afrikaans by the author

23 Niyati Keni, *Esperanza Street*

24 Yuri Herrera, *Signs Preceding the End of the World*
translated from the Spanish by Lisa Dillman

25 Carlos Gamerro, *The Adventure of the Busts of Eva Perón*
translated from the Spanish by Ian Barnett

26 Anne Cuneo, *Tregian's Ground*
translated from the French by Roland Glasser
and Louise Rogers Lalaurie

27 Angela Readman, *Don't Try This at Home*

28 Ivan Vladislavić, *101 Detectives*

29 Oleg Pavlov, *Requiem for a Soldier*
translated from the Russian by Anna Gunin

30 Haroldo Conti, *Southeaster*
translated from the Spanish by Jon Lindsay Miles

31 Ivan Vladislavić, *The Folly*

32 Susana Moreira Marques, *Now and at the Hour of Our Death*
translated from the Portuguese by Julia Sanches

33 Lina Wolff, *Bret Easton Ellis and the Other Dogs*
translated from the Swedish by Frank Perry

34 Anakana Schofield, *Martin John*

35 Joanna Walsh, *Vertigo*

36 Wolfgang Bauer, *Crossing the Sea*
translated from the German by Sarah Pybus
with photographs by Stanislav Krupař

37 Various, *Lunatics, Lovers and Poets:
Twelve Stories after Cervantes and Shakespeare*

38 Yuri Herrera, *The Transmigration of Bodies*
translated from the Spanish by Lisa Dillman

39 César Aira, *The Seamstress and the Wind*
translated from the Spanish by Rosalie Knecht

40 Juan Pablo Villalobos, *I'll Sell You a Dog*
translated from the Spanish by Rosalind Harvey

41 Enrique Vila-Matas, *Vampire in Love*
translated from the Spanish by Margaret Jull Costa

42 Emmanuelle Pagano, *Trysting*
translated from the French by Jennifer Higgins and Sophie Lewis

43 Arno Geiger, *The Old King in His Exile*
translated from the German by Stefan Tobler

44 Michelle Tea, *Black Wave*

45 César Aira, *The Little Buddhist Monk*
translated from the Spanish by Nick Caistor

46 César Aira, *The Proof*
translated from the Spanish by Nick Caistor

47 Patty Yumi Cottrell, *Sorry to Disrupt the Peace*

48 Yuri Herrera, *Kingdom Cons*
translated from the Spanish by Lisa Dillman

49 Fleur Jaeggy, *I am the Brother of XX*
translated from the Italian by Gini Alhadeff

50 Iosi Havilio, *Petite Fleur*
translated from the Spanish by Lorna Scott Fox

51 Juan Tomás Ávila Laurel, *The Gurugu Pledge*
translated from the Spanish by Jethro Soutar

52 Joanna Walsh, *Worlds from the Word's End*

53 Nicola Pugliese, *Malacqua*
translated from Italian by Shaun Whiteside

54 César Aira, *The Lime Tree*
translated from the Spanish by Chris Andrews

55 Ann Quin, *The Unmapped Country*

56 Fleur Jaeggy, *Sweet Days of Discipline*
translated from the Italian by Tim Parks

57 Alicia Kopf, *Brother in Ice*
translated from the Catalan by Mara Faye Lethem

58 Christine Schutt, *Pure Hollywood*

59 Cristina Rivera Garza, *The Iliac Crest*
translated from the Spanish by Sarah Booker

60 Norah Lange, *People in the Room*
translated from the Spanish by Charlotte Whittle

61 Kathy Page, *Dear Evelyn*

62 Alia Trabucco Zerán, *The Remainder*
translated from the Spanish by Sophie Hughes

63 Amy Arnold, *Slip of a Fish*

64 Rita Indiana, *Tentacle*
translated from the Spanish by Achy Obejas

65 Angela Readman, *Something Like Breathing*

66 Gerald Murnane, *Border Districts*

67 Gerald Murnane, *Tamarisk Row*

68 César Aira, *Birthday*
translated from the Spanish by Chris Andrews

ALIA TRABUCCO ZERÁN was born in Chile in 1983. She did an MFA in Creative Writing in Spanish at New York University and holds a PhD in Latin American Studies from University College London. *The Remainder*, her debut novel, won the 2014 Chilean Council for the Arts prize for Best Unpublished Literary Work, and was chosen by *El País* as one of its top ten debuts of 2015.

SOPHIE HUGHES is a translator from Spanish with a particular interest in contemporary Latin American literature. She has been the recipient of a British Centre for Literary Translation mentorship and residency, a PEN Heim Literary Translation grant and in 2018 she was announced as one of the Arts Foundation 25.